Motown Man

by Bob Campbell

UFP Fiction Series
Three Fires Confederacy
Waawiiyaatanong ✦ Windsor, ON

First Edition. October 2020

Library and Archives Canada Cataloguing in Publication

Title: Motown man / by Bob Campbell.
Names: Campbell, Bob, 1964- author.
Description: First edition. | Series statement: UFP fiction series
Identifiers: Canadiana (print) 20200286919
            Canadiana (ebook) 2020028696X
            ISBN 9781988214399 (softcover)
            ISBN 9781988214429 (HTML)
Classification: LCC PS3603.A47525 M68 2020 | DDC 813/.6—dc23

Book cover design: D.A. Lockhart
Book cover image: "Youngstown - Wick Building (OHPTC)" by Jess (Flickr)
Book layout: D.A. Lockhart
Book Editor: Maeve Keating

The UFP Fiction Series is a line of books that showcases established and emerging voices from across North America. The books in this series represent what the editors at UFP believe to be some of the strongest voices in both American and Canadian fiction writing.

Published in the United States of America and Canada by

Urban Farmhouse Press
www.urbanfarmhousepress.com

Printed in Abode Garamond Pro

For Wanda and Jonathan; and parents, Clarence and Rose.

K*eep in mind I hold no hard feelings toward happiness. I trust that it feels the same toward me, not that that really matters. It just doesn't work as a union. We're too different, at least at this stage in our existence.*

The strange, and perhaps beautiful, thing about happiness is it doesn't require some kind of ceremony or legal action to join with it. It's as easy as declaring, 'I'm happy.' Never mind if it's usually accompanied by or attached to some contrived reasons. It's still an identity that's as easy to don as slipping on a coat.

You know how these folks you meet talk about finding God and religion, then reinterpret 'the word' as often as necessary to conform to their worldview, no matter how twisted? That's happiness for you. And it's just as easy to remove or disassociate yourself from it.

The lack of a relationship with happiness leaves me open to experience life differently. Oh, sure. I have needs and desires that I wish to fulfill. And having done so would give me some satisfaction, temporary or longer.

But what it wouldn't do is make me beholden to happiness.

"Why am *I* here?"

It's a question he'd heard in some variation time and again; something he'd even asked himself more than once. He furrowed his brow and his eyes went searching for some version of truth.

Rays of bright afternoon light stabbing through parted, vertical blinds warmed the noiseless room. The sun's warmth inside belied the temperature outside. A fierce cold wind had swept down out of Canada and laid bare his true feelings about this so-called winter wonderland: *It sucks!*

He turned inward, sighed, and tried to re-engage.

Bradley had another stop to make before home.

With the gas needle pressed to E, he was running on fumes as they say. There were at least a few gallons in the tank; more than enough to complete his run of errands.

Still, he could already hear Abby's subtle objection: *Why do you drive around on E so much?*

He pulled into the station just up the road a ways from his sub-division in Grand Heights, parked at a pump island near the road, and got out.

Snow fell heavily and he squinted amid the swirl of large flakes. A trail of footprints in the fresh layer of snow followed him across the pavement as he strode toward the building.

The stop had only within the last few years morphed into a self-serve fuel plaza from the more intimate full-service station it had been, to better serve an influx of more people like him.

A young man exited the building as Bradly approached the entrance. A quick chin-up head nod—that sly way brothers silently communicate fellowship—was offered before the strangers looked past one another. The young man made haste through the snowfall to a nearby idling car—a tricked out maroon Toyota Supra—and vanished behind its smoky windows.

Bradley noticed in an instant the curb appeal of such an automobile even though it was, by then, several model years old. Nimble, sleek, stealthy, and un-American cars like that weren't simply a threat; they were the enemy. The people who'd dare drive one in this town were traitors—fucking traitors. Especially those who collected a weekly check from the major employer here.

How could one dare to bite the hand that nourished it? It was beyond comprehension.

Bradley scrapped those ideas, though. He had worked in the shop long enough now to know the occasional autoworker who had opted for a Japanese, or possibly German car, embodied something else other than simply being a "fucking traitor." What exactly?

He settled finally on freedom. They were driven by different ideas and inclinations; individuals, some of whom felt misplaced in this life. To Bradley, they were "Yobs", named for that Martian baby mistakenly delivered to the Earthling couple after a cosmic collision sent the two newborns to the wrong planets in that old Merrie Melodies cartoon. These people were certain it was in their DNA to do something else other than sitting at an assembly line for eight hours a day—five, maybe six days a week, or seven—if the plants were really pumping, making a wad of cash doing mindless tasks.

So to quell the frustration and longing to accomplish in this life what they were truly meant for, the Yobs drove Toyotas, Nissans, or the occasional Bimmer here and there. It was their way out of here, not unlike the Martian baby in that homemade spaceship of his, and they didn't give a rat's ass about what their union comrades or company men thought of them.

The pursuit of happiness: it's what made this country great. *Right?* And their choice of automobile was an individual declaration of independence. For these people were now cosmopolitan, professional and, above all, unbeaten in their stylish, well-engineered foreign cars. Instead of looking like an overpaid shop-rat behind the wheel of a lackluster Buick.

Bradley trudged on across the whitened asphalt to make his way inside to pay for a fill-up.

Monday

Them that's got shall have

1

Bradley had awakened hours earlier than usual, his mind churning through endless hours of twilight sleep like a factory through the night—monotonous, slow, repetitive— chained to a machine doing the same thing over and over again. Yet he stayed put, finding comfort with the thought that sleep would come rescue him quietly from this fitful existence. However, it wasn't to be. A restful night eluded his grasp like a feather in a breeze created by his flails, and Abby wasn't there to calm his impetuousness. She was 1,500 miles away, leaving him the lone ruler of a suddenly vast queen-sized bed.

After lingering in the bed's warmth for longer than what might be considered prudent, he got up and placed both feet on the cool floor. He made quick work of the morning routine and was out the door for work without delay.

Bradley couldn't remember the last time it had been so cold in mid-autumn. But the radio announcer ruefully filled in the missing pieces, stating it was the coldest November 4 recorded in four decades—more than a lifetime ago for a man his age. The country was fresh off victory in World War II the last November 4 when the mercury lapsed into such territory; the city robust, vital, and cocky with its vast arsenal of wealth. A rising working-class city upon a hill, it was. A place where people clambered to be.

As he approached the factory, Bradley saw billowy clouds of white smoke and steam bunching up in the sky above a miasmatic amber glow that enveloped the parking lot. The smokestack emissions were always fullest on the frostiest mornings, he noticed.

"Is that a cloud-maker?" he had asked once. Nestled between

mama on his right and daddy to his left on the bench seat of daddy's black Chevy Impala. His childish question so many years earlier hung in the air like an audible thought.

"Um-hum. It sure is." Her response tinged with mirth and motherly affection. Mama knew. She smiled and looked ahead as they drove on in peace.

The boy, meanwhile, continued to study that belching smoke-stack, oblivious to daddy's soft snigger. His conclusion was perfectly logical, adult Bradley would tell Abby years later. If the city's enormous factories could produce the great machines of warfare and automobiles to take us damn near anywhere we wanted to go, he argued: "Why not clouds, too?" He knew better now. That magical, fanciful world filled with easy explanations passed away long ago.

So, too, had the city's reputation. No longer a lethal weapon in democracy's great arsenal, the town had become a blighted laughing-stock for many. Buick City—a place where the American Dream was crumbling and rusting away. A city so far removed from its glorious and arrogant past when it made America go places. Those days seemed almost mythical.

"Okay, can someone tell me how the original inhabitants of North America got here?" His high school history teacher, a decade or so earlier, tossed them a softball from a previously assigned chapter.

"In a Buick!" The answer blurted from the back of room that day was buoyant and confident.

Bradley laughed right along with the rest of his classmates that day. His teacher, a short, balding man with a chip on his shoulder, even cracked a wry smile at Marcus' smartass reply. The shops were hopping in those days, and a clown like Marcus had no worries because his future was assured. After graduation he'd follow in the footsteps of so many others and enroll in UCLA—the University of Chevrolet Line Assembly, a euphemism for the city's auto plants. Yes, he would enroll in UCLA and maybe play a little softball, basketball, or bowl in a rec league after work.

However, when Marcus reached the head of the line, good, old reliable UCLA had all but stopped admitting students like him, as jobs in the auto industry here faded away. Even though his class-mate's answer that day in school still cracked him up years later, Marcus eventually had plenty to worry about. Partly because of all those foreign cars that had taken the place of daddy's Impala. Partly because of the infiltration of automation to help the local factories compete. Partly because Marcus had never really given serious thought to doing anything else except biding his time while keeping his classmates amused. And the last he'd heard of the old class clown? The answer had become all-too-familiar in this town. "Man, these days," his brother, James, had told him, "that brotha's doing his comedy on the crack-house circuit."

For here and now in 1991, his once-muscular hometown was emaciating before his eyes like an old industrial giant on the pipe. And the sight of those creeping factory emissions that Bradley once imagined to be new clouds fresh off the assembly line made him shiver. A cold jolt of reality that winter was fast approaching. But who's to question Mother Nature's prerogatives, he thought, before muttering under his breath: "Hmph. Should've worn a hat."

The sprawling factory complex sat in the distance like a gigantic battleship in port. Bradley pulled into its immense parking lot, hopeful to find a spot close enough to the entrance to minimize his time outside. He inched his red Pontiac—the brand of excitement according to the commercials—through the full lot, searching for a space of his own. He lucked out on a slot relatively close to the gate after spotting a departing third-shifter moseying up the aisle to his vehicle. Bradley slid right into the spot once the pickup truck vacated the space.

To the factory floor he marched, following a long, slow journey up and then down two steep flights of stairs. For the arriving worker, the first staircase led upwards to a place once thought to be New Jerusalem for thousands of the city's flock who had migrated from the old country—places in Eastern Europe or the South—in search of something better. But after generations of enduring the monotony and drudgery, the summer heat, the dirt, the smell, the lack of natural light, and the ups and downs of a punishing industry, more than a few now viewed the place as a hellhole.

At the top of the stairs, workers encountered not Saint Peter, but a plant security officer who sat ghostly at his post and watched indifferently. The entering workers waved their badges at him as if flipping him off.

Past the sentry lay a one hundred-yard hike along an immovable gangplank that spanned the rail and salvage yards behind the factory. It traversed the space like an expressway slicing through a tired city, providing safe passage between life outside the plant and life within.

Not unlike most days, Bradley's trek was lonely and anonymous in the dimly lit corridor. A stark contrast to the end of a shift when hordes of reawakened workers stampeded toward the exit like a herd of oppressed people who have just been given a sixteen-hour furlough.

Just up a ways, Bradley saw a lone man emerge from the shadows, headed toward him.

Attired in all black in an all-American sort of way—black leather jacket unzipped exposing a silk shirt, polyester trousers, and scuffed Stacy Adams wingtips—the man pimped with cigarette in hand and chest pressed outward like a red-breasted robin.

Upon encountering three middle-aged women dragging into work several paces ahead like a small squad of war-weary troops returning to the front, the jaunty, would-be player asked: "Hi y'all ladies doin'?" Before they could ignore him completely, he added: "There's a man up there givin' all the lovely ladies a kiss on the cheek."

The player didn't bother to elaborate before continuing on his merry way past the tired trio and then Bradley soon thereafter. Yet for all his charm and swagger, the waddling women were not impressed. The collective non-response suggested a kiss on the cheek had little value.

"Kisses on the cheek, huh?" the red-haired woman muttered. "Shoot, I should be walking on my hands then."

Bradley heard the woman's two comrades squeal with unadulterated delight; as though it was the best laugh they'd had in weeks, if not all year. He laughed too, from his safe position at the rear. He avoided passing them, all old enough to be his mother, so as not to cause them any embarrassment by interrupting their moment of joy.

They continued onward while he exited at an off-ramp, slowly descending a second flight of steep stairs to the level of the factory floor. En route from the stairway, Bradley felt the swell of familiar sounds as he passed through a short, back hallway toward a swinging set of large Plexiglas doors.

Inside, hydraulic cylinders moaned with each extension and contraction of their pistons. Pneumatic screwdrivers whizzed and whined with the pitch of a dentist's drill. High-voltage electric motors whirred. Forklift truck horns trumpeted and scooters squeaked. The hum of the huge climate changers bolted in the steel trusses high above the grimy floor resonated like a squadron of C-130s skimming the treetops. Workers shouted over the cacophony as the sounds all blended together in an orgy of noise and activity. Though loud, dirty, and sometimes hazardous, to him the bustling scenes and polyphony of sound could have a certain verve and rhythm that was, at times, jazzy.

His route led him past rows of enclosed electric automatic tube-bending machines, each one roughly the size of double-stacked large coffins. The department was almost serene compared to a decade or so earlier when scores of men and women manned standalone workstations; bending those hollow metal tubes on small, manual presses into crazy sipping straws that delivered gasoline to a thirsty engine. In those days workers placed the straight, two-foot metal pipes into the die, one after another, before energizing the press with dual palm-buttons which ensured the operator's hands were clear of any pinch points before the machine engaged.

It was there where that nameless, voiceless man working at a frenetic pace—presumably to finish his production quota early or to catch up—so captivated teenage Bradley. A cigarette glued to his lips, the worker's arms and hands seemed to operate independently of his body like a drummer lost in a solo. His head bowed slightly, the man never stopped working even as he peered momentarily over the tops of his green-lens safety glasses, twice making eye contact with that young high school co-opt student sporting the crisp white shirt and skinny yellow necktie from Hughes & Hatcher department store. Whatever became of that man with the dangling cigarette and the cool safety glasses after those coffin-sized automated tube benders—designed by electrical engineers like Bradley—made that autoworker's job obsolete? *Who knows?* Bradley resolved long ago.

The volume further dropped as he made his way through the toolroom where the skilled machine repairman and toolmakers went about their tasks. Sometimes with the refined precision of a violinist;

other times with the heavy-handedness of a club-wielding caveman. Along the way he passed a shiny quarter that had been superglued to the floor and caused more than one unsuspecting chump to stop and try to pick it up. Each time he approached the tempting currency, he reminded himself: *Don't. It's a trick.*

The toolroom produced much of the tooling and dies used in the various manufacturing processes at the plant. There, the ceiling was much lower and skylights sat overhead. Like the factory's other skilled trades, tool-and-die makers were part of an exclusive, blue-collar, we-can-build-any-goddamn-thing fraternity that paid damn good wages. It was a haven for the good ol' boys, their sons and relatives, and others like them. Like all entrenched fraternities, getting on trades was helped immensely if you were connected to someone on the inside.

As the number of hourly-rate production jobs dwindled and the future became less certain, more and more people sought out ways to get attached.

Beep.

Jim rolled up quickly behind Bradley out of nowhere.

The engineer turned to greet the skilled trades' foreman just as the three-wheeled industrial-strength golf cart rolled to a stop.

"Hop on. I'll give you a lift."

"Thanks."

"Yeah. Sure," said Jim, who jammed a burning cigarette with a quarter-inch of ash back into his mouth. The years of nicotine, caffeine, and restraining his enlarged impatience had tanned his raspy foreman's voice.

Bradley stepped aboard and sat down on the rear seat, back-to-back with the trades' boss. The yellow scooter jerked forward under Jim's quick acceleration and they became two heads of the same coin rolling down the aisle. For the rear-facing Bradley, it was as though he was now traveling backwards through time.

A trades' boss needed transportation to keep up with his crew. Whose millwrights, pipefitters, electricians, welders, and unskilled laborers could be dispatched to any one of a dozen departments on construction projects in the plant's west-end like some kind of un-chained gang. Though a millwright by trade, Jim had crossed over some time ago and *went on supervision*. No longer one of the boys among the blue-collar brethren, he traded for a white shirt and became just another suck-ass foreman.

Jim could still play the game, though. Union solidarity, with its power of seniority and other levers, made it easy for a crotchety journeyman to teasingly tell him to go to hell sometimes—especially if the company was being stingy with overtime. But to those trades-men caught sliding back late from lunch who would dare laugh at the prospect of being written-up, his response was resolute with fake indig-nation—"You guys stop that laughing 'cause I'm the one who's got to do the paperwork."—which told everyone Jim's heart was in the right place.

Bradley had subbed in as a trades' foreman one summer as a college intern and was familiar enough with the terrain; the hazing and all. He thought such behaviour fostered an independence that bordered on downright insubordination at times. A strong union made it pos-sible. And in this one-horse town, the union was a Clydesdale.

So he kept his mouth shut. Mostly.

Besides, Delcorp Vehicle Systems was in a fight for survival and the great corporate mothership had begun to seriously rethink its long-time practice of keeping all the automotive-supplier business in the family. Rumors had become the plant's chief product and were churned out regularly about how the plant was destined to be sold, spun off, closed, or dynamited. Other companies could make the same products and components for much less. And they weren't unionized. So, their wages dropped lower and the workers didn't tell their foremen to kiss their ass, jokingly or not. Without question, the union was a thorn in the company's paw, forcing the giant beast to tread lighter.

Bradley was sympathetic of the autoworkers predicament and respected their tenacity, at least in theory.

Jim chuckled, breaking the silence as the two men scooted through the plant. He plucked the cigarette from his lips and asked if Bradley knew some guy named Pulaski. The name meant nothing to Bradley.

"He's a trades' superintendent," Jim said. "Ha, that cocksucker can be a real prick. But he's a good guy. I guess… He went to this Halloween party the other night dressed as a black hobo."

Bradley grimaced, hoping he hadn't heard what just did. "Excuse me?"

"A black hobo." Jim laughed.

Bradley contorted himself just enough to see if Jim was serious. As he did, he got a face full of factory stench—a medley of lubricants, solvents, exhaust, and mustiness—and felt the sting of cigarette smoke in his eyes. He squinted and sharpened his focus. The scooter zigzagged around forklift trucks loaded with raw or finished parts, scooters driven by other suck-asses, and the black and white bodies of pedestrians that filled the aisles inside the division.

"Yeah," said Jim, still amused. "He wore black shoe polish on his face and what not. And I guess he couldn't get much of it off come Sunday morning. So he couldn't go to church."

His voice was loud over the factory din and rushing air, his amusement undeniable. Except for the churning sounds of factory life, the men were again separated by silence. The scooter raced on before stopping in the spark plug fabrication area near Bradley's cubicle.

"Thanks," he said, hopping off.

"Yeah, sure thing, buddy."

Jim turned and proceeded to drive off. He had traveled a short distance before stopping again after hearing Bradley shout: "Hey?"

Jim turned and saw the young man motioning for him to stop. He threw the scooter into reverse and backed up slowly.

"Hey, let me ask you something." Bradley stepped toward Jim, meeting him before the scooter had come to rest.

"Yeah?" Jim's reply was quick with a manufactured cheerfulness.

"Were there any black people at that party?"

There. He'd said it. There was no taking it back now. He didn't want to. His words struck like a brick through a plate-glass window separating the inside from the out. With the slightest arch of his eyebrows and a half-cocked, mirthless smile stretched thin across his lips,

Bradley's cool expression said: *Well?*

Appearances can be deceiving. Though something of a late bloomer physically, the once college boy now stood a shade over six feet with a lean build. But his heart now throbbed in his throat and he felt the awakening of dormant butterflies in his stomach.

Jim was rough-hewn in manner and dress, with small rump roasts for forearms. The foreman was built like a rook but the engineer was braced with resolve.

Bradley swallowed slowly to control his breathing and to push his heart back down to its anatomically correct position.

Jim's back stiffened. His expression flipped. He cleared his throat and his right eye twitched as a crimson tide washed over his fat head and thick neck. Jim's big hands gripped the steering wheel a little tighter as though he were trying to negotiate the bends on a dangerous stretch of highway.

"No, uh, I don't think so. I don't know really. I wasn't there." The words tumbled from his lips. "Another guy told me about it this morning, but he didn't say anything about any bl-*acks* being there."

Bradley hung on the way Jim said "bl-*acks*." That subtle emphasis on the "*acks*" by some whites. The speaker gagging on its mere utterance, the enunciation signaled a thinly veiled contempt for its racial connotation. It was choked out in statements like, *You* bl-*ack guys have big cocks*, and bl-*ack sonabitch.*

"Eh," Jim chuckled, "you know, I hope I didn't offend you or nothing. You know I didn't mean anything by—" He shrugged, as if to say, *Oh, well, fuck it.* He reached for a crumpled package of Merit cigarettes in his shirt pocket.

Bradley's face smiled before he spoke. "I was just curious."

Any thoughts of a rumble right there on the dirty factory floor dissipated quickly. There would be no blows exchanged because otherwise reasonable men don't have fistfights at work, unlike on T.V. The disappointment each man felt was palpable by the brief, awkward silence that followed. No, there would be no blows exchanged but there wouldn't be any communion either. And each man prepared to leave with what he carried.

"Well, thanks again for the ride."

"Sure thing, pal," said Jim.

"Yeah, sure."

Bradley turned and strode toward his cubicle. The foreman scooted away in the opposite direction.

2

Bradley's coat dangled on a hanger on the wall of his cubicle. The makeshift closet also included a hat rack—for those days when he wore a brim—and a small vanity mirror, which he faced.

Tearing at his tie, he fumed about the black hobo costume and at the superintendent—a superintendent, a fucking unclassified salaried employee!—for his audacity.

The nerve! To hurl such insults—*What did God say after He created blacks? Oops, I burnt one*—and expect shared laughter and camaraderie to ensue. Yet, to deny the blue-collar select—or any of those motherfuckers for that matter—of what some considered their birthright was to risk exile to the land of darkness, exempt status stripped along with one's latitude, such as it existed. The holiday privileges revoked, as Martin is transmuted into Malcolm.

Bradley had bitten his tongue so often it felt as though he had scar tissue for taste buds. People like his brother were far less forgiving. Still, was this the price of his modest success? His willingness to go along; his so-called tolerance of such folly? Mastering that way of being present and accounted for without really being there? All of him, that is?

No, not particularly. It didn't take much convincing, even if the math supported the theory of accommodation. Yes, he often found himself outnumbered but low-key is who he was. So, he rarely complained aloud. Each morning he rose, shaved, knotted his tie, and reminded himself over breakfast of what mattered most. And yet more times than he cared to recall, this had been his reward.

He was certain the guy wouldn't have worn such a costume if

he thought a black person might have been present. Bradley didn't know Pulaski but was confident that he neither socialized nor worshipped with people like him.

But why a black hobo with a counterfeit complexion, no less? He pictured how ridiculous and offensive this Pulaski guy must have looked in his *Birth of a Nation* getup. Pitch-black, with pale skin encircling his white eyes, creating the illusion his eyes were bigger and bugging more than perhaps they already were. Surely, Pulaski gave his buddies a little show on Saturday night. He must've asked for a quarter or two to buy a bottle of Wild Irish Rose. No doubt Pulaski's cohorts obliged his little charade and the truly generous ones probably gave him a dollar, if he asked them real nice like. Of course the show wouldn't have been complete without an expression of faux indignation by some asshole who wondered aloud why the black bum didn't get a job and quit relying on handouts from the working man.

If he wanted to be a truly funny black man, why not Richard Pryor? Anything just to demonstrate we could laugh together, that it wasn't anything so negative or personal. But it was personal, Bradley concluded. That's why the guy did it.

And of Jim, he thought: *Yeah, fuck you, too!* What did Jim expect? That they would share a laugh and instantly become boys allied against that cocksucker, Pulaski? There was no hint of shame or embarrassment in his re-telling. It was an ax wielded as some kind of imaginary payback. Payback for having to hire more blacks on skilled trades? Payback because the plant and city seemed to be dying a slow, painful death. And white people, it seemed, those like Pulaski and now Jim, felt they needed a face—a black face—to blame? All of the above?

Bradley chuckled. He caught a glimpse of himself in the mirror and, together, the two faces shared a laugh.

"What am I doing here?"

Delcorp was fighting for its survival, not unlike Buick City itself. But was it still his fight, too? Was it ever? Bradley had convinced himself that if a homeboy didn't jump in the brawl, who would?

As a high school co-opt, he had heard some vague but big talk about revamping an obsolete assembly operation to improve quality and efficiency while reducing the numbers of hourly workers in the process. Planners at the drawing board even noted how job losses could become problematic for organized labor somewhere down the road, an issue to be dealt with at another time and place. Between eavesdropping on conversations among the industrial engineers, filing papers, and doing other menial tasks to expose himself to the wonders of automotive engineering, Bradley never really considered that he could one day be a mate on the never-ending voyage to greater efficiency and lower production costs. It wasn't his calling.

He instead envisioned himself a master builder; the Frank Lloyd Wright of a new generation. More than anything else he wanted to design and build his own home someday. Bradley yearned to learn more about what it took to design buildings and communities. After unearthing the nerve to call a local architectural firm one evening to maybe offer himself up as a gofer or something, a tired, gravelly voice on the other end of the line told him that he didn't have anything set up to accommodate a wide-eyed high school student. But he wished the young man well on his dreams. *Click.*

Maybe he should have tried somewhere else. But he didn't. Something stopped him and that was that. Moreover, this town built cars and trucks and sparks plugs and air filters and fuel pumps.

Slowly his course changed. Maybe it was his interest in stereos that did it. Years ago he had gone to check out a stereo shop somewhere over there on the eastside of town, affectionately known to some as "Little Mississippi." The twenty-something-year-old clerk was gracious, though dubious of the boy's wherewithal to afford the store's expensive equipment. The spring day warm and sunny, but business was gloomy as the city was experiencing a downturn that foretold of worst things yet to come. The clerk must've figured: *What the hell?* So, he invited him back into the listening room where he proceeded to demonstrate the sound capabilities of different systems with some of his favourite tunes.

"This is one on my favourites," the clerk told him, as he lowered the needle to the spinning disc. He then passed the LP cover to his musical protégé.

Examining the cover was a revelation. That's *Jimi Hendrix?*

Bradley was certain he'd heard a song or two of his elsewhere without knowing who made it. But he liked it a lot. The sound spoke to him in inexplicable ways. The whole experience that afternoon was supernatural. Even though someone spewed a guttural "*NIGGERRRR!*" at him from a passing car a short time later as he waited at the bus stop, reminding him where he was and making him anxious for his connection to arrive, Bradley continued to dream about one day of owning a nice system where he could listen to Jimi in peace.

He returned home and began work on building his own system. He picked up a used Pioneer receiver from a downtown pawnshop. And he lucked out on some old hi-fi speakers housed in an ancient television-stereo console in his grandparents' basement. The speakers included two woofers, two midrange-sized and two smaller ones, for the higher frequencies. Alone in his grandfather's garage, he built cabinets made of particleboard and plywood. The cabinets he covered with contact paper to give them a wood-veneer finish. He spray-painted the speaker-mounting board a matte black like the speakers he saw in *Stereo Review*. Then he bought a ready-made crossover circuit from Radio Shack. The crossover circuit, he read, distributed the various electrical sound signals to the appropriate speaker. He also read the cabinets needed insulation inside to absorb the sound waves and minimize distortion. So he lined the walls with bats of foam rubber taken from an old seat cushion. Once he got the speakers all put together, the damn things actually worked. They also weren't just scribblings in a notebook.

He eventually saved enough money to buy a stereo turntable. He then set his sights on a tape deck. On a hunch, Bradley decided to wire his portable cassette player into his receiver. To do that, he surmised that he could split signal from the headphones jack and route it through the dual input jacks on the receiver for a tape deck. It was back to the mall and Radio Shack to buy a circuit splitter, a slim cable that resembled a snake's forked tongue. His makeshift tape deck worked just fine for the time being for his growing stereo system.

Impressed by his grandson's ingenuity, granddad suggested that maybe he become an engineer. *Yeah, sure. Why not?* Yet had Bradley known better, he might have called it for what it was—a means to an end; a way simply to get closer to the kinds of things one fantasizes over.

His proverbial first piece of ass instead turned into a long-term relationship. How could he resist? His interest in stereos; the exceptional grades; his aptitude and temperament—it all just sort of melted together. Meanwhile, his high school guidance counselor, who had taken a special interest in her young, gifted and promising black student, had begun cooing in his ear "everything is going electrical." The seduction began to overwhelm him.

Then there was the high school co-operative experience. At a time when thousands of local autoworkers were collecting unemployment while others packed up for Texas and the community began to seriously consider the possibility of life without so many factories, Bradley worked part-time after school as an engineering gofer in the industry. Although continuing the program at such a dire time seemed odd, he accepted the work gladly, the experience and the biweekly cheques that came with the assignment.

It was transformative. There, while working at Delcorp, he consummated his change of heart. But he wasn't merely a pallet being dragged along an automated assembly line from station to station to be fitted with the equipment to get him through life. No, he said, that's not how it happened. The choices were instead his to make after some sober teenage analysis.

His listened dutifully when his self-appointed mentor, a young black engineer who had done time in Nam, cornered him by the Xerox machine to dole out some soul-brotherly advice.

"Is it true that you served in *Vietnam*?" Bradley had asked, first; his focus elsewhere. "See any action?"

"Saw enough." The vet's cool, terse reply and stare chilled the kid completely. Bradley then saw more closely the keloid scar on the man's neck just above his collar that appeared to descend deeper toward his chest. His mentor, meanwhile, told Bradley to focus instead on the way forward.

"'Cause look here, young brother. There are a lot of places you can end up but there ain't a better place to start than right here. Consider yourself fortunate; very fortunate."

Bradley got the message. And when he heard the one about the man who came home from the bar drunk one night, a joke shared with him in confidence by another engineer—a much older white guy with a bushy mustache who sat nearby—Bradley was hooked.

Bradley had heard him re-tell a portion of the joke to a colleague only moments earlier. The colleague had heard it before but had forgotten the sequence of certain events. He wanted to get it right, no doubt, so he could pass it on to the next guy. Midway through the re-telling, the colleague remembered the ending—interjecting, "Oh yeah. I remember the rest now."—and left with an impish grin.

The old engineer returned to his work, only to be interrupted again by the kid from across the way who had ventured with a question of his own: "How did that go?"

The somewhat startled, older man looked up. "Excuse me?"

"The joke. How does it go?" The young man smiled nervously.

The old engineer smirked before glancing quickly out the left and right corners of his eyes. He motioned for the kid to come closer. The two generations met somewhere in the middle of that narrow passage separating the rows of metal desks in the open-air office. The old man's voice was furtive.

"A man comes home drunk late one night and staggers into the bedroom. He looks and sees his wife lying on the bed, asleep on her back. Her mouth is open. So he staggers into the bathroom, opens the medicine cabinet, gets a bottle of aspirin, and staggers back into the bedroom. Standing over his wife, he opens the bottle of aspirin, shakes out two tablets, and then drops them into her mouth. Well, the tablets cause her to gag and choke. She sits up quickly, coughing and spits out the aspirin into her hand. She looks at the aspirin and then at her husband. 'Aspirin?' she says. 'What? I don't have a headache.' 'Good,' the husband replies, 'Let's fuck.'"

The young man laughed, jubilant with his apparent acceptance into the club. The sage smiled knowingly and approvingly, then returned to his paperwork.

Bradley went back to work, too, but not before he caught a glimpse of a nearby department secretary, a woman who had taken a special liking toward him, glowing with motherly satisfaction from across the room. Embarrassed, Bradley cut his eyes away and erased the grin.

The middle-aged black woman had no knowledge of the conversation that had just transpired between the two males. But with that sideways glance and shrewd, crooked little smile, she must've known it was likely something naughty. Something about boys being boys, and that he—her surrogate son at the office—was now one of the boys, too. When it came time to choose a college, the choice was easy. He would attend the institute tailor-made for up-and-coming automotive whiz kids that was located right here in town. He could also remain close to family while continuing to learn and earn some money through the school's built-in co-opt program.

It was a mostly satisfying arrangement, to be sure, for a kid on the cusp of manhood facing a world of unknowns.

Now assigned to this lonely outpost of a cubicle on the factory floor, he felt something other than fulfillment. Bradley sighed and slid off his tie so as not to soil it or get it tangled in the machinery.

It was coffee time. En route to the community coffee station he passed by an old spark plug assembly line, one of a dozen obsolete lines soon to be replaced by the automated system taking shape across the aisle. A large rotary table was positioned at the head of line where a short, squat woman sat plucking the stenciled and glazed spark-plug insulators off the spindles one at a time before loading the parts into an iron tray.

Using her left hand as if playing a harp, she delicately picked each part off the revolving table with her thumb and index finger, and shifted it back into her pudgy, little fist. She had perfected this pinch-and-grab method to the point of being able to read her Harlequin novel simultaneously, never missing a beat. Once she accumulated five insulators in her left hand, she transferred the bundle to her right. The left hand returned like a typewriter carriage and resumed the plucking sequence. She then paused her reading and quickly inspected the fistful of insulators for any imperfections before loading them into the tray.

Bradley noticed how she and her fellow co-workers did it the same way hour upon hour, day after day, proving that factory robots really weren't anything new.

Two industrial-strength percolators—one containing caffein-ated brew, the other "unleaded"—were housed in a heavy gauge sheet-metal cabinet that resembled a small, green armoire. The sign said twenty-five cents a cup. But Bradley stuffed a five-dollar bill into the padlocked cash box, good for unlimited refills for the week for himself and the one or two thieves who betrayed the coffee honour system. Unopened cans of coffee, packages of Styrofoam cups, sugar, non-dairy creamer, plastic stirs, and paper hand towels were stored in the lower half of the cabinet.

It was a neat little set-up. He once calculated the coffee care-taker netted about two-hundred-and-fifty dollars a week operating his little concession stand. And the armoire was obviously a *government job*—that is, any task performed by a skilled tradesman that resembled real work but was really for a non-business purpose.

Once upon time, Bradley thought it mattered that company resources were being misused in that way, to say nothing of the rarely-seen guy who was a making a tidy profit peddling coffee on company grounds. Now, he only cared that the coffee was hot, fresh, and cheap.

Back at his desk, Bradley unlocked it to retrieve his pocket pro-tector filled with red and black ink pens, a mechanical pencil, a small ruler, and small regular screwdriver he used to open electrical control panels when the electricians weren't around. The skilled tradesmen were extremely guarded of their turf. They didn't want an engineer picking his nose without one of them being present to ensure it wasn't in viola-tion of the union contract and a nose-picker's job wasn't threatened. The electricians were the bitchiest of all, especially since an increasing amount of their work involved programming.

He unlocked the hutch over his desk and raised the door to reveal a variety of programming manuals and a framed picture of Abby lounging on the grass in the shadow of a silver maple tree. After stuffing his shirt pocket, he reached for the half-empty box of Marlboro Lights.

Bradley lit a cigarette and blew out a plume of gray smoke. He then took a swallow of coffee. The combination of nicotine and caffeine felt good against the back of his throat. He hit it again. He leaned back in his chair, his posture projecting an air of contentment, as though the nation's Civil Rights gods and goddesses might be gazing down upon him approvingly.

His eyes, however, fixed themselves on the burning embers of his Marlboro Light, watching the cigarette's white paper wither and darken before dissolving slowly into ash.

3

Hurry up and wait. Bradley cracked a wry smile as he privately mocked a favourite saying of the Delcorp tradesmen.

He sat in front of an industrial-strength computer terminal reviewing the program for a new automated assembly machine. His electrician counterpart, Gary—the so-called muscle of the team, Bradley sniped—would arrive at any moment and, together, the two-man crew would resume debugging the machine's elaborate program.

Gary was a stout journeyman electrician who, unlike some of his older comrades in the trades, embraced the new manufacturing technology. He did so not because he was such a great believer in the power of advanced automation, but because there was little choice. So many factories were being lost to the "Orientals and Mexicans," he said, that automation was the only way to compete for those jobs. Electricians had two choices, he told Bradley over coffee. They could shy away from the technology and become nothing more than "well-paid wire-pullers," or they could involve themselves in the newer technology. Gary chose the latter for himself, even if his heart hankered for the days of the good ol' boys.

Presently, their challenge was the binary circuitry that controlled a pick-and-place robot. An automated transfer process that moved a raw spark plug insulator from one revolving turntable to an adjacent one rotating in the opposite direction. The gripper-reflex maneuver essentially replicated the actions of that squat woman operator studied previously. Each table moved in synchronization with respect to the other—a relatively simple task, at least in theory. Still, the number of lines of sequential logic the operation required continued to fascinate him.

A programmable logic controller, a PLC for short, directed the multiple processes of the machine. It was the brains and its program was called a ladder diagram because the schematic resembled a ladder. The program's hard copy was Bible thick and it read like one, too. It dictated specific actions and reactions under a given set of pristine conditions. Though tedious and time-consuming, debugging and the related mechanical adjustments assured that the machine would actually function in an imperfect world. With six new lines slated for installation by project's end, work would remain plentiful for some time for some people.

Nevertheless, one step at a time, he reminded himself whenever he encountered a glitch with the ladder diagram.

The project was vital to the company's position in the global marketplace and something of an urban renewal tour de force. A large area inside the plant had been gutted and re-painted. Gone was the drab industrial green walls and machinery, replaced by brighter, richer colours—hues of orange, blue, and tan. The stained and grimy concrete floor had been resurfaced with a lustrous, gray epoxy finish; charcoal, black, and white acrylic flakes embedded throughout. All of this was done before the millwrights dragged and pushed the new high-tech machinery into place, to eventually displace an array of expensive, high-maintenance women and men.

The costly makeover was supposed to reduce manufacturing costs and improve part quality. But all that money and effort couldn't rid the old factory of its mustiness. It hung around like the ghost of greatness past.

Nonetheless, figuring out how to transfer small spark plug insulators from one turntable to another as smoothly as possible was the key to their future.

Yes, that was the idea.

Above the hum of the chaotic rhythms of the factory floor, Bradley's telephone rang out like a school bell over a noisy playground. "Bradley Cunningham." To the listener on the other end, it sounded as though his voice was a notch or two below a bellow. But the caller was used to his loud talk at work.

"Hi there, sweetheart."

"Hey. It's good to hear your voice. How are you? How's the seminar?"

"Okay. And class is fine. We started out this morning with a quiz—a diversity quiz."

"Diversity quiz?"

"Yeah. It had a series of questions about present and future demographics. You know, stuff like that."

He was silent.

"The seminar focuses on the communication styles of different groups of people and is supposed to increase our *cultural competencies.*" Abby chuckled, realizing she was beginning to sound like a diversity-training sales rep. "They say the melting-pot model is hopelessly flawed because it never included non-whites. And white women were included only to the extent that they understood their place in society."

"Okay. Well, did you pass?"

"Of course. I'm an advanced student."

The couple shared a laugh as the conversation paused; the factory's background noise filled the speech void.

"Listen, sorry we didn't talk long last night after I got here. But I was tired from traveling all afternoon and just wanted to rest. You know, I don't fly well at all."

"It's cool. Really."

"And then the flight. I don't know. For a long time, I just couldn't get comfortable. And I hate airports. All those people scrambling around while trying to prevent unpleasant thoughts from entering their minds. I hate riding in planes for long periods of time. The seats are so small."

"Well, last night you said the flight went okay."

"The flight was mostly smooth, I guess, and peaceful," she said, as she began replay portions of the conversation from the night before. "The muffled conversation and movement of the flight attendants helped me relax a little."

"Mm-hmm," he said, shuffling some papers on his desk.

"But then as we're making the final descent into Miami, the sky turned dark and ugly. And it was so quick too. That was the scary part."

She continued as if thinking aloud while Bradley faded further into the background of the factory noise.

"Conversation in the cabin stopped when the pilot ordered the flight attendants to take their seats. That's when I felt completely alone. The flight attendants are my lifeline. I figure if they're up were moving around, smiling and tossing out pillows and pop and peanuts, then everything must be okay. The pilot said it might be a little rough going. I could barely hear him for all the static. It made you wonder what else on the plane didn't work right. And you know seatbelts are like an absurdity on an airplane."

"No. That's not true," he offered.

Unconvinced and barely cognizant Bradley had said anything at all, Abby continued.

She recalled looking up and across the aisle out the window to her left, then the one to her right. Droplets of water sliced across the windows, and the plane's wings bounced like an empty diving board in a thick fog.

"The landing was really scary," she said.

"I could feel and see the plane teetering as it broke through the fog. And I could see the ground getting closer and closer. Finally, we're gliding over the runway until—*Bam!*—the landing gear hits the pavement. I watched the terminal go skidding out of sight."

Bradley chuckled.

"When the pilot welcomed us to Miami, conversation inside the plane switched on like a clock radio in the morning. I know this sounds silly," she said, snapping out of it. "It's not that I'm afraid to fly, but sometimes you just feel so, I don't know, helpless."

"It's called a phobia," said Bradley, "and you have it. But you'll get used to it. It's like riding a bus, with wings."

He chuckled.

"Huh?"

"I said you have a phobia when it comes to flying."

"No, I wouldn't say that."

"But look at it this way. It's still the safest way to travel. The numbers are on your side."

"Yeah, I know. I know," she said, unconvinced. "Maybe I'm just a control freak? Is that what it is?"

He chuckled. "I gave you my diagnosis. But I'm gonna love you anyway."

"Oh well, thank you sweetheart. Well, I guess I should get back inside. The troops are amassing again. We're learning all about Native Americans this afternoon. I can't wait. Call you later. Love you. Bye."

"Love you, too. Bye."

Abigail Larsen had wasted little time making a name for herself when she joined the *Daily News* fresh out of college. Her best quality, editors remarked, was her curiosity and willingness to engage it with accuracy and proficiency.

Still, her choice of occupation surprised many people given her rather reserved demeanor. To those who said they couldn't imagine her being pushy and shoving a microphone in somebody's face—like that former classmate who was jockeying for a date—Abby politely corrected them, stating that she used a notebook and not a microphone.

"It's all those obnoxious TV reporters who think they're Mike Wallace that give us all a bad name," she'd told the hopeful suitor. And no she wasn't interested in having dinner sometime but appreciated the offer.

If she wanted to, perhaps over dinner or drinks that never happened, she would have told him good journalism isn't all about getting a quote. It's about telling a story to give readers a better understanding of their world. It's not about a knee-jerk reaction to an event; it's about connecting the dots. Yes, that's it—connecting the dots.

When one of the city's largest hospitals decided to relocate to one of the affluent suburbs she covered, that was big news. Hospital executives and industry experts called it a strategic move because the greatest population growth was occurring in that part of the county. Maybe so. But the new location was also well away from the social problems of a decaying city. No need to worry about paramedics bringing the casualties of the inner-city struggles way out there to a beautiful health-care campus.

She recalled that prior to the hospital's announcement, there had been some interesting land transactions in the township where the hospital was headed. Turns out, several people with connections to the hospital's top brass had bought up large chunks of property in an area adjacent to the future site of the health-care campus. Now with the move certain, land values in the surrounding area were climbing nicely. Meanwhile, the stable middle-class neighbourhood soon-to-be abandoned by the hospital faced a less prosperous future.

Abby, along with another reporter, explored the potential impact of the hospital's move in a series of stories. It was that desire to connect the dots that led her to produce her best work to-date. The stories went on to win third-place for general news from the Michigan Association of Journalists.

The saddest part, she thought, was the project was still going through as planned. The attitude of the executives and much of the community at-large to the stories seemed to be "big deal." Still, she liked to think their effort provided a little better understanding of how we got into this mess in the urban areas in the first place.

She reasoned the growing separation between people, so often along racial lines, and mostly between blacks and non-blacks, was why diversity training evolved. And, she discovered, the failure to bridge these great divides were often as evident in the newsroom as anywhere else in society. The news media talked a good game, but more often than you'd think, many journalists were just as clueless and blasé on these matters as civilians.

That was part of the inspiration for the newspaper's "goin' back to the hood" campaign, as some reporters called it. The newspaper hoped to conduct one-day bus tours of surrounding neighbourhoods, industries, schools, and shopping centers for staffers to help better acquaint them with the various communities and put them face-to-face with readers. The trips included people from the newsroom as well as advertising and circulation employees.

Most reporters saw it as nothing more than a PR gimmick. They felt if people didn't want to read the newspaper, then they're idiots. They'll be out of touch. Staff writers also felt it breached the barrier between editorial and business operations.

As a cub reporter right out of J-school, Abby might have felt the same way. Now, she wasn't so sure. She tended to accept the views of the editor and publisher in that the effort might help better connect the staff to the community.

However, following the inaugural tour the newspaper found itself the subject of an unflattering portrait. The shuttle bus motored through downtown across the river and continued north up MLK Avenue, a thoroughfare stretching from the city's core to its northern edge like a bent bicycle spoke.

The other side of the river was simply the northside. For many readers of the *Daily News*, it was so distant a place it could have had its own dateline:

Northside — Two men were found shot to death yesterday in an abandoned house.

The northside was another way of saying nigger, Negro, coloured, Afro-American, African-American or simply, black side of town. Not black as in *black is beautiful* or *being in the black*, but black as in *black Monday, black market, black-balled, Black Death*, or bl-*ack guys with big cocks*. Black: the realization for many whites of a nightmare come true. The northside: what you get when there are too many blacks gathered in one place; the embodiment of an affirmative action plan gone awry.

Yes, Abby knew the story well.

"Okay, everyone lock their doors," the nasally voice of a young male had called out during that trip. The barb, later pointed out in a mandatory staff meeting, was greeted with a few coughs of laughter from other members of the entourage.

The artery had been renamed King Avenue several years earlier to commemorate the slain civil rights leader, perhaps with some misplaced optimism that a name change would pump new life into the street. Yes, some argued, the prostitutes and crackheads would overcome.

Many residents were still waiting for the avenue to get to the Promised Land, however. Despite the presence of a few well-kept, reasonably stable areas along the corridor, the string of dilapidated and burned-out houses, boarded up buildings, liquor stores, and overgrown, trash-strewn lots is what stood out in the minds of most. An affront to King's legacy, they said.

The newspaper's small group of black reporters were particularly amused by bus tours. At lunch when no non-black person was around to hear, they jokingly referred to that part of the excursion as "African-American Country Safari."

"Go into the jungle and see it for yourselves. Up close and real," said one, widening his eyes to frighten the others at the table. From that day forth, the name stuck among the small band of black journalists.

The safari very nearly caused a tribal war within the newsroom and left the editor refereeing his own staff. Gerald Yates, who had an uncanny ability to tower over taller people, was staggered by the discord among the staff he so proudly shepherded.

A community transplant with not quite a year under his belt as editor-in-chief, he desperately wanted to believe the bond he shared with these men and women was genuine and felt equally throughout the newsroom.

Instead, Abby concluded, the episode painfully revealed what he and others perhaps knew in their hearts: If a "bond" existed, it did so on opposite sides of the rushing river separating blacks and whites.

The incident and its aftermath showed just how fragile the relationships were among those who labored each day side-by-side, like soldiers fighting an invisible enemy by day and partying in separate tents at night. The dissension lingered in the building for months, masking once familiar faces with shades of suspicion.

When the shuttle bus was hit with empty forty-ounce beer bottles, it shattered the illusion of oneness in the *Daily News* newsroom. Worse, it suggested that perhaps their craft wasn't a special calling after all, but merely a factory where people assembled a product made of ink and paper.

The episode marked the first time Abby—who wasn't on the trip—felt compelled to choose sides. It had been relatively easy until then.

The bottles smashed into the shuttle van just below a passenger window on the left side where two white guys were sitting.

No one knows why they did it. One could only guess.

The bus trip had paused near a tiny lake in the northwest part of the city near the site of an old amusement park. The thrill rides had been dismantled decades ago and well before that trio of young men, seated in a clearing not far from where the bus had come to rest, had taken their first breaths. The bus was there several minutes and perhaps the boys thought the passengers were talking about them. One apparently decided to give the tour group something interesting to talk about.

Some staffers thought the bottles were thrown only to mess with the bus' mostly white occupants. A few on the bus said the group appeared to have had a good laugh at their expense. But others called it an act of hostility, possibly fueled by race. *Why else would you throw an object at a bus?*

Who knows, really? No charges were ever filed.

The incident produced a news brief, including a photograph of the damaged vehicle. The black staff was incensed about the coverage of a petty crime the paper would otherwise ignore. Management and staff also debated whether to continue the little journeys. Many whites said no to the forced busing.

Meanwhile, the paper's black columnist opined about the incident before extolling the virtues of the fact-finding missions. She also reminded readers of an incident that happened months earlier where several young white men hung a scarecrow over a bridge onto the expressway at night as part of a sick Halloween prank.

A motorist, startled by what she thought was a person standing on the highway, ran off the road as she swerved to miss it. She died of a broken neck after being tossed from the car as it flipped.

The columnist wrote:

Was it an act of hostility? Or was it simply a stupid prank that went too far? More importantly, should we now avoid the area at night and be wary of young, suburban white males?

In the end, the bosses decided to continue the newspaper's community outreach. The worst part of the tour was over anyway.

Some white staffers huddled among themselves and complained minority interests had again buffaloed the newspaper's better judgment. Black staffers also shook their heads in disgust. The paper continued to publish, while the editor sought out a higher authority to reduce the newsroom tension.

The diversity seminar, which Abby now attended in Miami, was supposed to offer at least a partial solution. Her mission was to bring back the truth from Florida.

Abby wasn't the editor's first choice to represent the paper, however. He wanted to send a black person.

His first choice was the black columnist. But she declined, saying she'd be in Jamaica that week and wouldn't reschedule to be a part of the *Daily News'* hand-wringing exercise.

In turning down the assignment, the outspoken commentator stunned her white boss when she had told him flatly: "It's you white people who have the most trouble with this diversity business. Why don't you go? Or send a white reporter and see what they think. Because y'all better learn what it feels like to be a minority. It'll come in handy later. Your day is coming. Trust me."

The editor bristled at her sassiness, though he said nothing. He didn't have to; his face said it all. But the challenge was too great for the former college debater to ignore. He was determined to go forward with diversity training.

He also wanted the newspaper represented by a reporter for the newsroom's perspective. So he asked Abby, who he privately considered to be a future candidate for an editor's job. The experience might also be useful in her current job covering county government and local politics, he explained.

Abby was hesitant to accept the assignment. She dreaded the thought of air travel to and from the conference, though she kept her fears to herself. She also thought the wrong person was being asked to attend.

She figured: *Why not—*

And that's when it hit her. Something else was going on. Was she being asked to do this because she was *engaged to a black guy*? Did that somehow make her uniquely qualified for this assignment?

"Look," Yates had said quickly, as if reading her mind and trying to prevent those ideas of hers from blooming. "I understand if you don't want to do it. I can ask someone else." He eyes shifted elsewhere momentarily. "But I'd really like for you to consider it. Think of it as a favour for me."

A favour? For a brief moment, she sensed a different energy

emanating from that stocky, little man. It passed quickly.
She agreed to do it.

What does it mean to be black?
Barbara Walters put the question to Barbara Jordan during one of her face-to-face television specials in the late 1970s. The question had always stuck in Abby's mind. What does it mean to be a *black* American?

She had long since forgotten Barbara Jordan's answer but never forgot her own reaction to Barbara Walters' question. Walters' audacity both thrilled and sickened her. How many whites have been asked on national television what it means to be white? She wondered.

This was in the pre-public backlash period over race-conscious remediation programs, like affirmative action. The seemingly halcyon days before a growing number of whites began to rethink their liberalism. Before deciding that being white in America meant being a victim of reverse discrimination by employers, university admission officers, and organizers of the Miss Black America pageant.

Back then, defining whiteness (at least publicly) was the exclusive province of the Ku Klux Klan or some neo-knuckle-draggers. Everyone knew *those* people were on the fringe of society and sanity. So the subject was off-limits for other white people, like herself.

Abby, though, imagined herself being asked what it meant to be a white American. She wrestled with it, trying to pin an answer. There were false conclusions.

She first decided that white equals privilege, but later scrapped the idea. That might work in the good old South, but not across the country because there were too many whites on welfare for it to be true. So, she figured, whiteness cannot be just about class status because that can be changed, despite what some might argue to the contrary.

An adequate explanation escaped her, that is, until she began dating Bradley seriously. That's when she resumed her private inquiry into the meaning of whiteness.

After observing the differences in the way merchants treated her when Bradley was at her side versus the treatment she got when he wasn't, the pieces slowly began to fit together.

Perhaps whiteness, she thought, was akin to an American Express card: *You don't want to leave home without it.*

Yes. She liked that. Whiteness, she decided, is tantamount to absolute security from an identity standpoint because you don't have to think about it; you don't want to think about it. You don't have to worry about going certain places and wondering if you'll be hassled simply because of your skin color.

Sure, you may be hassled for other reasons, but you're able to deal with those conflicts as separate and distinct issues with the idea a resolution may be entirely possible. So, for instance, if you stop screwing my boyfriend, bitch, everything will be fine. A person can be completely rational in such a dispute. That makes it simple. It's deal or no deal.

But how do you tell someone to stop being black?

Yes, she concluded, the essence of American whiteness means not having to think about being white.

Whiteness is Lady Liberty, the ultimate symbol of freedom. It had profound implications. School integration, for instance, sounds good but is laced with practical problems because it forces whites—students, parents, teachers, and administrators alike—to think about being white.

As her theory continued to evolve, she reasoned that suburbs aren't really about property values, good schools, and low crime. At their core, the suburbs are about rigid sameness. The perception of absolute security in knowing your neighbour is just like you, so much so that you don't have to think about it. Why, it was almost fascist.

Abby accepted the Florida assignment out of the belief it was for a good cause and that the odds favoured a safe round-trip. She thought, too, it would be something of a mini-vacation and give her time to put some other things into other perspective.

Bradley was skeptical of this diversity-training jazz. He resented the notion that blacks and black culture was reducible to something resembling a freshmen survey course or a chemistry class for non-technical majors. But he didn't say that. Instead, he asked: What can you really learn in a week that you don't already know? And what then? "I don't know," she had said. "Guess I'll find out, huh?"

In the weeks between accepting the assignment and the day of her flight, Abby began to share her fiancé's doubts about the long-term value of such training. It does sound funny, doesn't it? she thought.

The night before her flight, Abby dreamed the *Daily News* was closing, joining the list of newspapers around the country that had folded, and leaving her to seek employment elsewhere. It was terrifying. What else was she really qualified to do, she wondered.

I could always become a flack, I guess, her unconscious self answered.

4

Monday evening, Abby dined alone in her hotel room on food delivered by a Hispanic attendant who spoke with a thick accent and smiled easily. After dinner, she watched a pay-per-view movie before calling her sweetheart to wish him goodnight.

As she drifted into sleep she thought how comforting the queen-sized bed felt without someone else trying to annex the extra space or, while resting in the arms of Morpheus—the ancient Greek god of dreams—not having to negotiate silently with that other person for more blanket and space.

Hours before she called, Bradley had made plans to dine alone at their favorite restaurant—an Italian bistro near downtown.

He drove east out of the subdivision—one of those residential pods that use to be known as neighbourhoods—and headed towards the interstate that sliced through the heart of town. It was part of the same northern route he followed to work each morning; the same high-way that, when it was built, cut the heart out of the city's oldest black neighbourhoods. However, he stopped first at a convenience store for a pack of smokes.

He craved a cigarette earlier in the evening but had left his pack at work out of habit. He generally did his smoking at work.

Abby didn't care for cigarettes, even though she knew he smoked sometimes behind her back. She tasted it in his kisses. Now, with Abby away, he could indulge his appetite after hours.

"Pack of Marlboro Lights, please."

"Two dollars," said the clerk, who slid the pack across the counter after the money changed hands.

"Oh, could I also get a pack matches?"

The clerk, in mid-puff of his own cigarette, hesitated briefly before tossing him a book of fire.

"There you be, chief," he said, barely looking up. "Five cents."

Bradley gave him three pennies and took two from the penny tray beside the cash register.

Outside, stripping the pack of its plastic cover and tearing open a corner, he dug into the package pulling out a cigarette. With a square hanging from his mouth, he fumbled with the small book of matches before finally generating a spark. He cupped his hand around the flame, crouching his head and shoulders so the wind wouldn't disrupt his pleasure. He inhaled and blew out a mixture of smoke and steam into the cold night air.

As he headed towards his automobile, Bradley saw in his windshield the reflection of the clerk who seemed to have been watching his every move.

At the entrance of Lazio's, Bradley held the door open as an elderly couple exited the building. He couldn't help noticing the deep wrinkles in the woman's aged face. She had the skin of a person who'd spent too many unprotected hours in the sun. The couple thanked him as they strolled slowly past.

Inside the lobby, he waited for the hostess to seat him. The attractive young woman smiled warmly as she returned to the station.

"How are you this evening?" Her high, full cheekbones gave her face the allure of one who's easily amused. The eyes were engaging, and her skin looked healthy and moisturized. "Just one tonight?"

"Yep. Just me," he said.

"Right this way. Non-smoking, right?"

"Yeah," Bradley replied. "Well, on second thought, give me the smoking section."

"Oh. Okay. Let's go this way then."

They changed course and headed left. The hostess motioned for him to have a seat before placing a menu in front of him. "Your server will be right with you. Enjoy."

He watched a female server tend to a couple who had apparently arrived only moments before he had been seated. She then swept pass him with a quick step while tossing out that she would be right with him.

She returned a short time later with a basket of bread and asked if he was ready to order.

"What are your specials tonight?" he asked, with restrained annoyance at her truncated routine.

"We have a Tuscany pork and pasta dish. It comes with pork tenderloins sautéed with tomatoes, wine and basil, and that's served over a bed of penne pasta. We also have pasta and Prosciutto with peas. That's served with fettuccine, Prosciutto ham and snow peas with a chicken stock sauce. Finally, there's the olive chicken Parmesan. It a boneless chicken breast on fettuccine with black olives, onion and basil. All three are $12.50 a piece, and it comes with a house salad."

"Which do you recommend?"

"They're all *really* good," she said.

Bradley settled on the Tuscany pork and pasta, and ordered a glass of Chianti.

The restaurant was cozy. The décor featured checkered red-and-white tablecloths on an assortment of small tables and booths. Bottles and canisters of olive oil adorned the shelves along with artificial breads, dried garlic bulbs, and paintings of the old country.

Operatic wails illuminated the background. The small place was about half full.

Once the meal arrived, the server returned twice to his table—once to deliver a second glass of wine and once to drop off the check. The hostess returned with Bradley's credit card and the receipt for his signature.

"So where's your girlfriend tonight?" Her white, cotton shirt was unbuttoned suggestively yet stylishly low to expose her moderate cleavage. Her hair was bobbed, and the scent of her rosy perfume tickled his nostrils.

"She's away at a conference all week in Florida," said Bradley, noticing again the sex appeal of this woman before him.

"Florida? Oh, that explains it. She left you here all by yourself to freeze. Awww." Her eyes flirted. "I bet she's enjoying the weather."

"Yeah, well, she said it's been raining the whole time. She left Sunday."

"Rain? Awww. Booo. That's no fun."

He signed the receipt, adding a customary fifteen-percent gratuity to the bill. He didn't feel the server had earned it, regardless of society's conventions on that sort of thing.

But waitresses come and go. He liked the place and the hostess especially. She alone justified the tip. The foreign and mysterious lyrics of an Italian love song playing in the background aroused in him a passion for her:

I palpiti, i palpiti sentir!
Confondere i miei co' suoi sospir.
Cielo, si puo morir;
di piu non chiedo, non chiedo
Ah! cielo, si puo, si puo morir;
di piu non chiedo,
si puo morire,
si puo morir d'amor

Bradley bade goodnight to the hostess and briefly entertained a fantasy of taking her home with him. He then promised her he'd return.

On the drive out, he listened to Coltrane blow out the notes to Moment's Notice on the evening jazz program from the local public radio station. He thought again of the hostess and muttered, "Yes, on a moment's notice."

Bradley continued on to his house in Grand Heights.

Tuesday

Them that's not shall lose

5

M r. Coffee pissed into his thermal urinal as Bradley unlocked the front door to retrieve the daily gazette. The unseasonable Arctic chill transformed his breath into small bursts of steam instantly with each exhalation as he stepped off the concrete path into the frosted grass.

The carrier had again missed the welcome mat by a wide margin. The folded newspaper instead lay hidden between two dwarf juniper shrubs in a dormant flowerbed where bouquets of yellow marigolds and red begonias blossomed from spring until the first killing frost.

Only the din of distant interstate traffic ruffled the tranquility of the immediate block. A subdivision trying to become a neighbourhood in a township masquerading as a city. The character hadn't changed much since he moved in several years ago. Curved and twisted avenues plowed through the retired acres of farmland defined its passing charm. Aged elms and towering maples that provided sun-splattered shade in the summer and piles of dead leaves for work and play in the fall did not stand here. Miniature trees instead dotted the residential landscape. Trees that if felled would reveal few rings of history on their stumps, suggestive of a community unshackled from the past. The sky was wide open.

Abby joked the subdivision had the permanence of a Monopoly board sprinkled with identical plastic green houses and red hotels. To his brother, James, it was the vinyl-clad, two-car-garage embodiment of light jazz. "A community designed by Kenny G," he said.

Bradley understood it hadn't matured to the point where kids played touch football or kickball or foursquare in the middle of the street, games that paused only briefly to allow a car to pass through or for the occasional time-out for water and peeing. No hopscotch played on those sidewalks; there weren't any sidewalks. No hide-and-go-seek played here at twilight where much of the street, including the bushes in the neighbours' yards, was a potential hiding spot. No, community property did not exist in the old way.

Indeed, she thought. The subdivision was a subdivision of private parcels on which sat neat, mid-sized houses built for couples on the go to nowhere in particular, except for maybe another subdivision with larger homes and plots. Subdivisions where kids had organized adult-supervised activities and playdates to keep the streets clear, and Sega and Nintendo video games to teach them how to play ball, drive fast, or kill bad guys in virtual reality.

Abby and Bradley roosted there because Bradley bought the house before the engagement. The new construction satisfied a longing for something different. The blueprints reminded him of the homes and buildings he once designed in his dreams. Nice neighbourhoods still existed in the city but he wasn't interested in someone else's hand-me-down or financing another family's flight out of Dodge. He wanted a bathtub that no other butt had sat in and a community that belonged to him as much as it did to his new neighbours. After reading in the newspaper that new homes were sprouting in fresh soil, he set his sights on Grand Heights.

Bradley was there from day one when the foundation was poured. He dropped by week after week wandering through the jungle of two-by-fours as they took root on the sub-flooring to form the exterior and interior walls. He watched carpenters work back-and-forth like a typewriter carriage, slapping on then fastening the shingles. He delighted in the echoes of the virgin space of the enclosed, empty structure.

Homeownership – the right thing to do for an up-and-coming young man of means. Stable property values and good schools also translated into greater resale potential down the road. Later, other advantages emerged, like watching earnest, young working women and stay-at-home moms jog or power-walk in Spandex shorts and sweatbands. Their bouncing tits and ponytails made for a pleasant sight after a day of work and weekend mornings. Except for the occasional visual delights that Bradley privately partook, not even a skeptical journalist could question the subdivision's other attributes all that much.

When Abby decided to unload her baggage there, who could quarrel with two bathrooms, walk-in closets, and bedrooms you could still move around in after they were furnished? Besides, she figured it was only temporary.

Bradley picked up the newspaper and brushed away the dirt and frost. As he did so, the red rubberband holding it all together snapped loose and disappeared into the earth. The freed newspaper appeared to stretch as it began to unfold. He used the occasion to scan the front-page before stopping at an article in the upper right corner.

A local man had been arrested after firing several shots at a fleeing car outside his home on the city's northside. The shooting was in apparent retaliation for an alleged armed robbery that had occurred just moments earlier.

Bradley, dressed in trousers and white T-shirt, was momentarily oblivious to the frigid air as he moved toward the door. His movement seemed driven by automation, never looking up while skimming the top-of-the-fold article, which included a photo of the alleged shooter looking rather matter-of-fact at the scene of the crime.

Inside, Bradley sipped creamed coffee and read on.

The man told police three men, one armed with a semiautomatic pistol, approached him as he prepared to leave for work Monday afternoon. They left with his cash, several pieces of jewelry and other items.

The alleged shooter, who works second-shift at the truck plant, said he was loading his car when out of nowhere a midnight blue Buick Century, with the three young men inside, stopped at the end of his driveway.

"Excuse me, sir," said a man in the front-passenger seat. "I'm

looking for an address."

No, the victim told the reporter, he didn't know the men.

"I guess they had me at 'sir.' Next thing I know, there's a gun pointing at me. Man, I froze. You see what I'm saying?"

Standing at the edge of his driveway, where his property ends and the public right-of-way begins, he was told to "check in" his wallet, gold wedding band, diamond-studded pinky ring, gold necklace with a charm, and lunchbox, too. The wallet contained eighty dollars in cash while the Igloo Mini-Mate stowed a recently purchased Sony Discman and headphones alongside his lunch for the day.

The robbers remained inside their vehicle during the course of the illegal transaction while carefully monitoring their victim's movements. With the misdeed done, the Buick Century departed the scene swiftly, according to the account.

Alone at last, the victim said he was now free to unzip his coat to retrieve the handgun lodged inside an interior pocket. He reached for it quickly as he stepped into the street and fired off shots at the fleeing car.

He told the *Daily News* he thought he'd struck the car at least once and saw heads duck down as it sped away.

"I guess I just sort of snapped, he admitted. "I was like: Enough! And I'll be damned if someone's going to rob me in front of my own house."

Asked why he hadn't brandished the weapon sooner once the robbery was in progress, he told the reporter:

"I didn't want to get shot! That's why. See what I'm saying?"

The bandits did not return. However, the police did arrive, called by a worried neighbour who reported hearing multiple gunshots and "seeing or hearing" a car speeding away from the scene. Separately, the victim-turned-outlaw called to report an armed robbery.

Police then arrested him for discharging a firearm and carrying a concealed weapon and confiscated the gun. Meanwhile, the prosecutor's office was weighing whether to charge him with assault with a deadly weapon and possession of a firearm in the commission of a felony. Vigilante justice is inexcusable, he said.

"It's one thing to protect yourself, your family or your property from harm. It's quite another to take the law into your own hands and pursue a suspect with guns blazing," the prosecutor said. "That's not how we do things in this city, in this county, in this state. Pursuing a criminal suspect in this manner is the job of a trained law enforcement officer, and I emphasize the words law enforcement officer."

"Enough," said Bradley, reciting the story's bold headline with an exclamation point. "Hmph."

Bradley shook his head with disgust. He dropped the newspaper and finished dressing for work.

6

A cornucopia of fruits, breads, donuts, personalized boxes of cereal, juices, milk, and coffee had been carefully and attractively arranged on the buffet table. The spread almost looked too good to disturb.

"... and thy desire shall be to thy husband, and he shall rule over thee," said Walter Montgomery, president of Montgomery & Associates, quoting Genesis 3:16. "And a fourth-century bishop, St. Ambrose, had this to say about male-female relationships: 'Adam was deceived by Eve, not Eve by Adam.'"

He paused to allow those borrowed words to burrow into the consciousness of those present in conference rooms D and E. Hearing no objections, he continued:

"Our bishop, therefore, concluded this: 'It is right he whom that woman induced to sin should assume the role of guide lest he fall again through feminine instability.'"

Montgomery smiled. "Feminine instability. Female creatures were deemed untrustworthy in certain situations. Your innocence and fragility needed to be guarded and protected by whom? The male animal, of course," he said, before anyone else could answer. "So you see, the seeds of gender conflict were sown in the Garden of Eden, where the mandate was established about the roles of men and women in civilization."

"But then who was it who said, 'I am woman, hear me roar?'" said Anne Riley, Montgomery & Associates' vice president. Her eyes panned the room like those of a patient fifth-grade teacher quizzing her students.

"Helen Reddy," said a proud, middle-aged feminine voice from the back of the room.

Scattered chuckles rose and eyes rolled to the ceiling.

"That's right. Yeah…Who said that? Okay. Great," said Riley, in a calm, soothing voice after identifying her star pupil. "Strong. Invincible. You know, these were terms never before used in public to describe women. These adjectives were reserved for men, usually white men. Right? Even though we knew better. We knew there were strong, independent women in our history, even though we were fed constant images of the submissive, dependent housewife. June Cleaver, right?"

Abby lingered on those last few words of the Montgomery-Riley spiel.

Abby knew firsthand that life was neither a 1950s sitcom nor an archaic fairy tale of white knights rescuing damsels in distress before living happily ever after. She would like to have seen that loving fairy tale couple once they had been together a decade or so. She recalled how her parents fought like animals, verbally assaulting each other. Those fights were usually about money, or so it seemed.

Alone in her room at night, she would seek out and isolate the sound of a cricket's chirp or distant traffic, a siren; anything to distract her from the sounds of mommy and daddy shouting at each other down the hall. Abby sometimes wondered if their bouts over dollars weren't really an excuse for something else. Maybe the real source of their domestic discord lay elsewhere, deep beneath the surface in the shoddy foundation of their shotgun marriage. Maybe her mother and father just didn't like each other very much and didn't know how to split gracefully. So they used fights over money, and trivial things, like a crowbar to smash the union. Whatever the cause, they finally did it and divorced.

Sometime before the courts and mutual dislike undid their vows, and days after a particularly nasty argument in which her mother finally threatened to leave and take her child with her, Abby's father confided something to her. "You know," he said, "your mother and I have had our disagreements. But never once have I hit her. Not once."

She heard sincerity in his voice and he seemed oddly proud, like maybe he was somehow better than his old man in that department.

He looked down at his twelve-year-old daughter who sat on the front porch of their home, hunched over hugging her knees underneath a blazing sun. Abby looked up and saw nothing but a shadow of a man against the sun's bright, white light.

Well, whoop-de-do, she thought but said nothing. She instead lowered her head and stared back at her bare feet, focusing on her blue-polished toenails and thought: *what a jerk.* She didn't understand then or care, for that matter, what it meant for her father to say what he said. She had no idea of the courage it must have taken for a grown man to try and explain himself to a child. The only thing she understood at that moment was she wasn't a princess living in an enchanted kingdom.

"Nevertheless," Riley said, her voice pulling Abby into the present, "out of these gender roles our society assigned, certain communication patterns emerged. And that's what we want to tackle today. Understanding how we, men and women, tend to communicate and respond differently to various situations in the workplace. To do that, we'll need to gain an understanding of the feminine and masculine cultures in our society.

"As we have said repeatedly during this course, the key to improving communication across these imaginary lines of demarcation, be it racial, ethnic, or gender, is to develop a greater cultural awareness," Riley said.

"Yes," said Montgomery, nodding in agreement as he stepped from the background. "We'll also briefly touch on sexual harassment in this section. Okay, then. Any questions before we move on?"

"Yeah, I have one. In talking about gender relations and sexual harassment, wouldn't touching be considered off limits?" said a man up front in the audience, prompting some laughter among his classmates.

"Oh, yeah. Right. No pun intended," said a smiling Montgomery, who added quickly after glancing at the guy's name tag: "Class, Tom, here, gets a gold star for the day."

7

Bradley stood before the open doors of the large, freestanding electrical panel, watching the columns of tiny light-emitting diodes flicker on and off. On, then off. On. Off.

To a casual observer, there wasn't any discernible pattern to all that blinking. The lights twinkled like tiny raindrops crashing into a puddle or maybe a silent, digital interpretation of Thelonious Monk's *Trinkle Tinkle*. But, in fact, there was a pattern; a rhythm, if you understood how the machine operated.

Bradley understood what was going on. The PLC that controlled those tiny lights, which registered an array of electrical inputs and outputs, had lost its run light. Worse, the run light had failed to illuminate despite multiple restart attempts by the maintenance electrician.

He knew the electrician's shorthand method well: You cycled power, which meant disengaging the electrical panel's main disconnect—a giant light switch—waited a few moments and re-engaged it. Do it a few times if necessary, and, sooner or later, run light returned. Usually.

Fortunately, at that moment the run light glowed red with its devilish one-eyed stare. That meant an orderly flow of operational sequences was occurring; information being processed again, with inputs generating meaningful outputs. That meant parts out the door and money in the company's cashier register.

Input equals output equals input equals output. That simple equation was once again a true statement. And so on. And so on.

Cycling power was a quick fix; like pressing a reset button. Why it failed in the first place was hard to fathom—too hard, it seemed—for a maintenance guy whose primary task was to keep production flowing and on-time.

Microelectronic malfunctions were invisible to the naked eye and often required sophisticated diagnostic equipment, time, and patience. And all three were often in short supply on the production floor. So, you cycled power and hoped to God the processor cleared its head and remembered what in the hell it was supposed to be doing.

When that simple, quick fix seemed to be failing, the electrician went looking for help. Yet by the time Bradley arrived on the scene, the electrician's one-last-try to get it going had paid off. The run light was lit and the line was clanking along.

That electrician then departed because first shift was ending and he wanted to get in a shower before a line had formed in the locker room.

Once he was gone, Bradley took out his pocket screwdriver, unlatched the panel door's safety catch, and opened the doors so he could observe the frantic LEDs while trying to read the mind of the beast.

That's where the second-shift electrician found him when he arrived on the job a few moments later.

"What's going on?" the tradesman asked.

The name *Steve* was stitched in white thread over the pocket of his maintenance uniform shirt, which was completely unbuttoned to expose the black Harley-Davidson T-shirt stretched over his bulging beer belly. His sleeves were rolled up to his elbows and the tool-belt hung off his right shoulder giving him a slightly tilted posture.

Presumably, the unorthodox manner of carrying the tool-belt gave him the aura of an undercover cop who carries his sidearm in a shoulder holster, unlike a lowly patrol officer. To Bradley, those macho skilled tradesmen looked like they were carrying a shoulder-strap purse.

What's going on? A loaded question, to be sure.

Steve wanted to know why this electrical engineer was nosing around his territory, poking his head inside an electrical panel without a proper escort; that is, an electrician. Steve and his cohorts thought the company was trying to get guys like Bradley more involved in solving certain types of factory-floor diagnostics, usually those involving process control devices like PLCs. Maintenance electricians feared they would be the most vulnerable if the company's rumored plan was ever implemented. That's why they challenged even the slightest trespasses of engineers.

Bradley acknowledged him with a quick glance and head nod. "Hey, how's it going?" he said then, as if pressing a reset-button on the exchange.

Steve said nothing, but stepped forward to peer inside the panel, and the two men stood side-by-side watching the electronic apparatus winking at them.

"You might keep an eye on this," Bradley instructed. "It lost its mind a couple of times this afternoon."

"Yeah, that's what the dispatcher said the first-shift guy told him. What did you do?" The monotone utterance belied his cramped disposition.

"I didn't do anything." Bradley faced the inquisitor; his stomach twinged. "Your first-shift guy cycled power several times, but it apparently didn't do any good. I was asked to come over and take a peek. But it was working again by the time I made it over. So there you have it. I guess you lucked out on this one." Bradley smiled.

Steve took a sip from the cup of black coffee he held in his left hand.

"Cycling power usually takes care of it," he said, after a swallow. "I'll stay here and watch it for a while. Maybe I'll re-boot the program. That sometimes does the trick."

"Yeah, that might help," said Bradley, who backed away from the panel and accepted the job was, indeed, a maintenance call and a minor maintenance call at that. "Let me know if you have any more problems with it overnight. I'm thinking about starting a log to track those machines that seem to be losing their run lights on a regular basis. One of the things we want to do in the new area is a better job of documenting our maintenance calls."

"Dispatcher does that now," he lied.

"Yeah, well, we'd want to keep track of all the maintenance problems for a particular machine by date, time, and malfunction. And the information would be kept right at the machine. I'd be interested in any ideas you might have on setting up something like that. Maybe it's something we can brainstorm on together."

Steve took another sip of coffee before giving a noncommittal nod and weave.

"All right then," said Bradley, "see you later."

"Have a good one," said the electrician. He then assumed the dominant position in front of the open doors of the electrical panel.

Bradley retreated back across the aisle to his cubicle. Realizing that it was also his quitting time, he unrolled his sleeves and grabbed his necktie. He tied a quick four-in-hand knot and slid the lump up close his open shirt collar.

He thought again about what might be causing the run light to fail sporadically. Yes, he knew what was going on; the real question was why.

It could be some kind of electrical disturbance that caused the program operation to malfunction. Maybe a starter coil for an electrical motor, or maybe the machine's motor, was back-feeding an electrical pulse that the PLC was misreading as a computer pulse. Maybe the PLC was picking up stray electrical disturbances from the atmosphere, which might require better shielding on the interconnecting cables.

Whatever the cause, cycling power was only good for so long. At some point somebody would have to find the source of the real problem.

As Bradley locked his desk and hutch, he reconsidered his exchange with Steve. He harbored no illusions of finding a note about the machine's overnight performance on his desk come morning. He was equally doubtful of the chances of collaborating with Steve on anything.

He switched off the desk lamp and headed for the parking lot. En route, Jim whizzed by on his industrial-strength golf cart, heading in the same general direction along a main aisle.

The two men acknowledged each other with a flash of eye contact and gentle nods but did not speak. Had they spoken, and under different circumstances, each man may have discovered something really funny—that maybe they actually had something in common. That maybe they genuinely liked one another. They instead continued on separately; two locomotive freights running on parallel tracks whose occupants were inaccessible to one another. Farther up ahead, their paths diverged completely.

"A local man is being hailed as a hero today. This comes a day after he took matters into his own hands when three men robbed him at gunpoint outside his home on the city's northside. But the county prosecutor says not so fast. The prosecutor is considering charges against the man who fired several shots at the fleeing suspects. There were no injuries reported. Meanwhile the robbery suspects remain on the loose."

The announcer's voice faded into the background as Bradley drove out of the parking lot toward the expressway.

He wanted the shooter, this victim-turned-outlaw, charged for his recklessness. He wanted the prosecutor to make an example of him. The law would be an instrument of the outrage he felt toward the suspected black robbers, the victim-turned-outlaw, the newspaper and stupidity everywhere.

Selfishly, and not unlike the way fickle fans cheer a referee's questionable call so long as it serves the interests of their team, he also thought the prosecution might help settle a contest that had erupted earlier in the day between Abby and himself.

Although incredulous, Abby was moved by the newspaper's account. She recognized the bizarre tale as a good news story. Her very words, in fact—that's a good story—when Bradley summarized it for her earlier that day.

She had asked who had written the article before answering her own question just as quickly: "Was it David Anthony?"

Her voice suggested that maybe this fascination with the double-crime story wasn't limited to just the facts but might also extend to the police reporter who had strung them together.

However, Bradley set aside that bit of intrigue and had proceeded to explain his dissatisfaction with the whole account.

"And I certainly don't think it should have gone on the front page with a headline like he's some kind of action hero or something. Here, with all the problems this city has with guns and all, the paper runs a story that basically glorifies the very thing it wants the rest of us to be so outraged about. This guy firing down the street could have hit anyone. Bullets land somewhere."

Abby tried to counter by offering a different perspective. "I'm not saying I agree with what the guy did," she had said. "In fact, I think it was stupid and very dangerous. But I do think it was a good news story. I'm glad to see the paper report stuff like that. I think the public has a right to know because—"

"Oh. Ok, here we go. You know what? Spare me that 'right to know,' stuff, alright?"

"What? What do you mean?"

His voice grew in volume, louder than necessary to cover the factory's background noise.

"That's always the answer for you guys: 'the public has a right to know.' To know what? That people do dumbass things? Well, stop the presses."

"Huh? Yes, that's part of it."

He continued as if he hadn't heard her reply: "Or that you need to be afraid of...of black guys? That we don't think rationally. That we're violent."

"What? Brad, why are we having this conversation? And why are you talking to me like I'm a stranger all of a sudden?"

During a lull in their edgy conversation, Bradley paused and exhaled. He looked up and saw Abby's framed picture on the shelf over-head. He continued: "I just thought the tone of the article and the fact that it was on the front page was way off base. You know, there were some things about it that just rubbed me the wrong way. Like why is it so important that this guy had a baloney sandwich and watermelon in his lunch box? I mean, c'mon."

Before she could respond, he added, "and I guess I was a little, I dunno, embarrassed."

"Embarrassed? Why?"

She had said it only to steady herself against the barrage of frustration that had been hurled against her, not to patronize. She knew damn well why he might feel embarrassed by the story, even if she didn't necessarily agree with his reasoning. Still, she suddenly felt like a wife who had forgotten her spouse's birthday.

He brushed past Abby's question—"Why?"—and instead asked

her a question. "Is the reporter black?"

"What?"

"Is he black?" he pressed. "Is the reporter black?"

"I heard you," she said, thinking again about the volume of his voice. "And would you please lower your voice? No. He isn't."

He was a white guy who was a pretty good reporter. But she didn't say that. Nor did she bother mentioning he was somebody who didn't have a stake in the city's future; that he was likely just passing through. Building a clip file the way so many other young reporters do before looking to move on elsewhere, to a larger, more prestigious newspaper.

It was the same game plan Abby considered when she came to the Daily News some years earlier, before she fell in love and moved into that house with the two full bathrooms, walk-in closets, and central air conditioning in that subdivision in that township masquerading as a city. And before an unacknowledged phobia further altered her trajectory.

"What's gotten into you all of a sudden?"

"Nothing's gotten into me," he snapped back, as the chances for a quick resolution and reconciliation dissipated. "I just didn't like the story. That's all. You know how I feel about those things and, well…"

"Well, what?"

"Nothing. Nothing. Skip it."

The noisy churn of factory life filled the void while they sat silent on opposite ends of the line.

"Look, I know you're outraged…and you should be. We should all be outraged by something like that," Abby said.

"Mm…yeah, I suppose."

It was then, like a feudal lord guarding his domain, Bradley eyed the young electrician, an apprentice, as it turned out, approaching his cubicle. He was looking for the journeyman electrician; said he needed a hand with a machine across the aisle that had lost its run light again. Bradley told the guy that Gary was gone but offered to go over and see what he could do to help.

"Look," he then said to Abby, "I need to get going. We can talk later."

"Okay."

"Bye."

"Bye."

The abrupt ending was just as well. Abby needed to get back inside where her class was about to resume its discussion of gender relations in the workplace.

But Bradley's question left her raw, stripped of a layer of her own identity. And, she thought: *How dare he trivialize my profession? It's the same one that so often championed the plight of the society's underdogs, in case you've forgotten.*

Perhaps she'd never be anything more than a mate with an asterisk beside her name; that she would be Bradley's white wife. She expected that from some people, black and white. But him too?

Bradley sped toward the city limits. He'd had enough of the radio and turned it off. On the freeway out of town, he pressed hard on the accelerator, racing pass other cars as the factory town became ever smaller in his rearview mirror.

8

The music heard outside Lucy's had a clarity and resonance that only comes from a live performance. Bradley liked to say that recorded music in a club is like macaroni-and-cheese from a box. No matter how much Kraft advertised their product as the "cheesiest", it simply could not match the kind of homemade, baked macaroni-and-cheese made by real people like his grandmother.

A short line had formed on the sidewalk along Champion Avenue where people waited their turn to see The Moses Redmond Band, a blues group that also played in Detroit, Ann Arbor, and Windsor. Moses was a favourite attraction at the club. Bradley liked them too; he liked to hear the blues performed live. Several other bands also played there from time to time. They were pretty good and crowd pleasers. Heck, most local bands are crowd pleasers because the music's live. But even on their best nights they couldn't match the power of Moses. This band was the real deal.

Lucy's was one of the few places in town that featured good live entertainment, at least at a joint he'd patronize. Bradley also found it was refreshing to see and hear brothers jam on real instruments for a change. Now, it seemed everyone wanted to be a glorified DJ or some kind of rapper. DJs had their place but he couldn't help feeling, at times, that something magnificent and indigenous to his people had all but vanished and been replaced with something coarser, less refined, and more derivative. The blues were an American treasure, so he felt some responsibility to help keep it alive by supporting bands like Moses Redmond. And on a night with Abby out of town, it was better to spend the evening with Moses and the boys than home alone in the suburbs.

The cozy little joint occupied space on a neat little boulevard that was also home to a bridal shop and an ice cream parlor with a sidewalk take-out window. And on a warm night, it was walking distance from his alma mater. Inside, the individual tables were so close one could participate in a conversation at a neighbouring table almost as easily as he could at his own. Two pinball machines stood like sentry posts at the opening of a long, narrow corridor that led to the restrooms. At the front of the room, just off the entrance, was a cramped stage that always seemed to be just the right size.

Presently, the brother playing the electric guitar had a grasp on that instrument as if he were choking it, making it wail and howl for sweet, sweet mercy. He seemed to be transferring his private torment, or pleasure, animating that object. Meanwhile, the faces in the crowd of twenty and thirty-something men and women yelped with almost sadomasochistic gratification, as if each one wanted to be that guitar man or his guitar.

Bradley felt peanut shells crunching beneath his feet as he slipped through the tiny fissures of the compressed crowd toward the bar where a wall of preppy, young white men stood like an attacking defense crowding the line of scrimmage. But because the long-neck beer bottles in their hands resembled small, brown billyclubs, the group had the ominous presence of a lynch mob.

He saw an opening along the line and squeezed through enough so as to grab the attention of an unacquainted barkeeper. Bradley ordered up a billyclub of his own and, beer in hand, moved away from the group to the rear of the room where he could observe everything. His back against the wall, his eyes bounced easily from the neon-trimmed beer signs above the bar to the nineteen-inch television set tuned to ESPN, to the posters featuring those sexy, ample-tit blond and brunette white babes wearing string bikinis or those tight, yeast-infection jeans. The guitar man struck up the band's next tune. The brother led off with a guitar solo before his boys joined in. Moses then stepped to the microphone and looked out over the blob of laughing and chattering faces.

"Hey, Joe," he sang, "where you goin' with that gun in your hand?" He asked again.

Bradley leaned against a pinball machine and stared back at the performer who seemed to be looking right at him. He held a swig of beer in his mouth a moment or two and swallowed.

Bradley and Abby sometimes went to Lucy's together, although it had become less frequent in recent months. The place had a tinge of naughtiness, or so he liked to believe, that was lost when you went there as part of a couple. The element of pleasant surprise was lost when your mate was on your arm. Everything seemed a bit too scripted, including the musical score and audience reactions. Nowadays, it seemed they only tended to stop by on those restless nights after having seen an early movie or dined out.

Lucy's was most enjoyable when he went there alone, which he did infrequently whenever Abby had to work the second shift for the weekend rotation at the newspaper.

This was the place where he had decided to make his move on that slightly older woman who was now slated to become his wife. Bradley had met her previously in the non-threatening surroundings of a cocktail party, hosted by a co-worker. Abby had shown up as the guest of a friend who was acquainted with the party's host. Across the crowded living room, Bradley's eyes kept bumping into Abby's. Like two associates known to each other only by their faces but whose paths continually cross in the office corridors. Abby remembered how he was the only black person there yet seemed perfectly at ease and in control. In spite of herself, she wondered what that must have felt like—to be the only black in a room full of whites. Bradley recalled how Abby glimmered with an aura of availability—a curious quality of standing simultaneously as a part of and apart from the crowd. She had large, outgoing eyes and smiled affably. When they found themselves alone on the third-floor balcony looking out over a manicured lawn bordered by an asphalt parking lot (actually, Bradley watched Abby venture outside and pursued her), it was as though those same two associates now found themselves standing in line at the copier and one finally decides to learn the name of that familiar face he'd smiled at so many times before. A connection made, it was just the beginning.

He said he worked at Delcorp as a controls engineer, speaking in a manner people in the know would understand. But her eyes told him she had never heard of anyone ever getting a college degree in such a discipline—control.

Meanwhile, she noticed his thin, graceful fingers, the glossy manicured fingernails, and his shoes. The stylishly neat brown oxfords with a coordinated leather belt, blue jeans, and white cotton shirt were a subtle fashion statement that guys she typically attracted rarely made. His afro was trimmed close and conservatively, yet featured a stingy tendril nibbled into it. And he smelled nice.

Wondering if this guy who was given to such fashion detail might be also gay, she had asked: "So what do you do?"

"Well, it varies. For instance, I debug new programs for machines, design electrical panels or estimate what size programmable controller is needed for a particular application."

"What are—"

"Programmable controllers?"

"Yes."

"I guess the easiest way to describe them would be to think of them as industrial-strength personal computers." He smiled. "But unlike your home computer, a programmable controller is a process control device for an assembly operation. And it communicates with the machinery through a series of input and output modules, or cards, as we call them."

Abby's output was a slow head nod after the receiving the crash course. "So, you have a degree in…electrical engineering?"

"Yes, that's right." He paused. "Real exciting stuff, huh?"

"No, I think that's interesting. Why would you say that? I'm sure it pays well. Don't you like it?"

"Yeah, I do. I really do. It's like a puzzle sometimes. I guess, too, I like having the freedom to roam around the plant at times. You know, I'm not chained to a desk so much."

"I mean, you're actually qualified to do something," she chimed, as if lost in thought.

"Excuse me?"

"No. No," she laughed. "I mean, you have a real skill and electrical engineers are in such demand. That's all. That's all I meant. Don't throw me off the balcony."

They laughed as it became clear something between them was

beginning to click.

When it was Abby's turn, she said she was a reporter for the *Daily News* and tried hard to speak as though it was really no big deal.

"Really? Wow. That must be interesting."

It garnered another no comment from Abby. She shrugged instead. He then mentioned how he enjoyed reading the newspaper, for the most the part.

"I'm glad somebody does."

Uneasy the comment might be a thinly veiled brush off, he sought clarification. "What do you mean?"

"Oh, I didn't mean it like that."

Her hand touched his arm as if to steady him. She worried it seemed at times as if newspapers were becoming passé.

"TV has taken over. Of course, there would be no TV news without us. But I like what I do," she added, quickly. "We reporters are writing the first drafts of history."

"Is that right?"

"I borrowed that from someone. It makes us all feel better."

They shared a laugh.

"Yeah, well, I guess that's true to some extent…So are you working on anything interesting? Or how does it work? I mean, how do you come up with things to write about?"

She smiled as if trying to contain a chuckle. It tickled her how many non-journalists often asked that question, as if she wrote fiction.

"What?"

"Oh, it's just that I'm not use to being interviewed. No. No, I'm only kidding. I'm only kidding."

She laughed and touched him again, this time her hand lingered a moment longer than before.

"Oh, so that's what this is? An interview?"

Abby explained how she had recently completed a puff piece on community heritage museums. He shrugged to indicate the jargon meant nothing to him.

"You know," she continued, "a story without any bite. They're meant to brighten the page up and show these suburban communities that we're paying attention to them, that they matter. See, it's all part of our focus on the greater metropolitan area"—her voice becoming sing-song—"since so many of our readers now live in the burbs. My editor assigned it. But there are far more interesting stories out there that I'd rather be covering."

"Oh yeah? Like what?" Bradley asked, as he took note of her slender face and lips.

"Those that will help the reader better understand the community they're living in. I like news analyses and news features. Stuff like that."

"Heavy-duty stuff."

"Yes. I mean, just look around you. This city has its problems, but it's a good news town. There's so much going here in a lot of ways. The whole de-industrialization issue is happening right here."

He nodded in agreement.

"You've got crime. You've got a downtown that's trying to reinvent itself. Neighbourhoods. Race relations…"

"Mm."

"In fact, the whole area is caught up in these issues, since the auto industry is so dominant here and all. I just think it's an interesting community in some ways, at least from a news standpoint. And the *Daily News*, it's a pretty good paper. I mean, it's not the *New York Times*. But it's decent."

"So, what you're really saying is that you want to be where the action is."

She smiled. "Well, yeah. I'm looking for some action." She joked.

Bradley chuckled under his breath, certain she was tipsy. "Well, I'm sure you'll get your chance, sooner or later," he said, finally.

Shortly afterwards, Abby was informed her ride was leaving, much to Bradley's disappointment. She had a hint of bitch that was strangely alluring. He felt cheated out of the opportunity to ask her out for a date, and he didn't want to rush a request at the moment of her departure. Days later, Abby still on his mind, he considered calling her at work but talked himself out it. A relative brief encounter at a party wasn't enough ask her out, he concluded. Maybe she was just being cordial. He also didn't want his call to be somehow misinterpreted. He had forgotten she had touched him during their initial conversation on the balcony, how she had breached the boundary of air separating them not once but twice.

But then came the chance meeting at Lucy's. It was a sure sign, he told himself and later Abby.

Bradley saw her across the room drinking with some girlfriends. Meanwhile, he was filling full of himself. His confidence was building on the strength of a secure future in engineering with the largest corporation in the world.

When a waitress swung by his post along the wall and asked if he would like another, he responded he would.

"I also would like to send that woman right over there a drink. Give her whatever she's having; whatever she wants. It's on me."

He stood by the pinball machines and waited anxiously for that drink to be delivered. Would she remember his face? Would she and her girlfriends share a laugh at his expense? Did she dig black guys? His heart pounded as he feigned nonchalance.

The waitress dropped off the package then turned to point out the guy standing with his back against the pinball machine. Abby's eyes followed the hand as if she were spellbound by a hypnotist's watch.

He stood there with at least eight pairs of eyes looking at him. He felt instantly paralyzed, but somehow managed to raise his bottle and smile.

Abby and her two pals turned and leaned towards one another to convene an emergency meeting of the security council. The image reminded Bradley of the Three Stooges holding an impromptu huddle in the middle of a blues club. And he imagined the conversation that ensued: *Who's the black guy? I'm not sure. What are you going to do? Should I ask him over? Where would he sit? It's too crowded over here. How come he didn't send us all a round?*

Then there were laughs all around.

Abby looked again at Bradley and smiled. She then got up and made her way over to the gentleman, walking sideways through the crowd as though she were tiptoeing along the edge of a cliff.

He tried not to sound disappointed when he said: "You don't remember me, do you?"

"Oh, I know who you are. You're that guy from the party. Yeah, the one who would read a story about community museums."

"Right…That's me."

"Well, thank you for the beer. We were trying to figure out who you were. It's kind of dark in here."

"I figured as much," he said. "You all sort of looked like the Three Stooges huddling over there."

She laughed, a very good sign, he thought. They chatted briefly, almost yelling into each other's ear because of the music volume. Both mentioned how much they liked Lucy's and live music. She thanked him again and continued on to the ladies' restroom before returning to the table to be debriefed by her friends. Bradley imagined debriefing her as well. But he left the bar that night still wondering whether Abby dug black guys.

The following Monday he decided to find out, not that it was his primary or even secondary aim. He just wanted a date and wasn't looking to conduct any social experiments. He had a name, her place of employment, and the department. The second meeting, the one at Lucy's, was the catalyst. But when his phone call finally found its way to what he thought was Abby's desk, an impatient male voice answered.

"Newsroom."

Bradley explained almost apologetically he was trying to reach Abigail Larsen.

"She's at extension 203. This is 206. I can transfer you. She's not at her desk, though," said the harried voice.

Bradley could hear the sound of frantic typing in the background. The fingers on the hands that belonged to voice moved like giant five-legged spiders tapdancing hip to hip on a computer keyboard.

"No, I'll call back."

Click.

He phoned again an hour or so later. This time Abby Larsen picked up. After a few throwaway comments, including a question about whether he had called earlier, Bradley said how nice it was to see her again and invited her to lunch sometime soon.

"Lunch? Uh—" Her mind scrolled quickly.

She saw her nosy neighbour, Derrick, the voice of impatience from the first call, glance up from his terminal. He had completed his editor's must-have story about a group of high school cheerleaders who had toilet-papered the wrong house—a story he protested as being a bullshit assignment. He was now keeping himself busy cruising the

Associated Press wires, looking for an interesting story to kill some time with before disappearing for the day.

"Oh, oh," he said then, nudging himself into the conversation. "Sounds like somebody's tryin' to Mack."

Mack? She didn't know what he meant exactly by that comment, but assumed it had something to do with the boy meets girl.

"Sure, we can do lunch," she said into the phone.

When Abby hung up the phone, Derrick smiled and asked: "Sooo, Miss Larsen, when's the big date?"

Two days later, they met for lunch at a so-called international marketplace, one of those contrived gathering spots that was anything but international but would surely enliven a morose downtown. More than the food or atmosphere, it was the locale that drew them there; something of a mid-point between their respective job sites.

"The night we met you said something I wanted to ask you about. But we got caught up talking about something else and I never got back to it," she said. "You said you like reading newspapers for the most part. What did you mean by that?"

"I said that?"

"Yes. What did you mean?"

He shifted somewhat uneasily, trying to recall making the comment. He was flattered she remembered such a tiny detail from their first conversation. Right then, his comfort level with her increased that much more.

"Hmm. Well, it's just that sometimes it seems like the media has a one-size-fits-all mentality when it comes to the way blacks are portrayed. You know, sometimes I'll see something and think, 'Yeah, that's okay. But that's all we ever see.' Or, I'll think, 'That's cool, but there's more to it; more to us, I guess, than that.' Does that make sense?"

Abby nodded slowly, her eyes were fixed on him. "Yes," she said. "It does. In fact, that's a real concern, that we don't do a good job of covering the black community…"

He hung on the words *black community*—another pet peeve— before deciding to let the urge to comment pass.

"…or women or other minorities or the suburbs, for that matter. Part of it," she continued, focusing again on blacks, "is the make-up of the newsroom. It doesn't reflect the racial make-up of the city. There's a guy I work with named Derrick—I think you spoke to him when you called—he's constantly fighting with the editors over stories. Uh, he's black, and I say his race," she added, quickly and rather apologetically, "only because it's germane to what we're talking about. Otherwise..." Her voice trailed off.

Bradley nodded to register acceptance of her explanation and that she didn't have to tell him Derrick was black.

"It's not just newspapers, though," he said. "It's a lot of places—commercials, movies, magazines. You know, there's this razorblade commercial that really irks me. It's advertised as a razor for the all-American face or the great American face. Okay? But the only faces you ever see are those of white guys. And I think, what's the message here?" He stopped suddenly and chuckled. He sat back in the chair and felt himself blush.

"Look, I don't want you to think I obsess over this stuff, because I don't. I'm not a militant or anything, but it's little things like that you tend to notice. And the newspaper, well, let's put it this way: my brother likes to say the media has never found a negative story about blacks that it didn't like."

She grimaced. "That's not fair. No, I don't think that's fair at all. Is that how you feel?"

"No, not entirely. But you guys, or should I say, the media has its moments, as I said before." He smiled.

"Well, we don't look at stories in terms of whether they're positive or negative, per se. News is news, so that's the criteria we use. It's what I use."

"Really? Well, I guess I do, sometimes."

She said nothing but her expression begged for clarity.

"I mean, I see some stories and think of them as being positive or negative."

"Name one."

"Well, I can't think of one right now, not off the top of my head. But let's look at this way: I could say there's no such thing as good or bad engineering, and that engineering is engineering. But if a bridge falls down, then you'll say it was bad engineering because most likely it was. Or look at the auto industry. The media," he smiled, "is always quick to talk about how poorly-engineered American cars are supposed to be, right?"

"Yes."

"Then how come news stories can't be classified as good or bad? Sounds like you guys are trying to have it both ways."

"Well, you began by saying positive or negative."

"Oh, so now you want to get technical," he laughed.

"Nooo," she nodded, "I'm not trying to get technical. Besides, most stories are done on things after the fact, after the event has already occurred. It doesn't change what has already happened. You can't blame the messenger. On the other hand—no, let me finish," she said, when he motioned to interrupt. "If that bridge you talked about was engineered right the first time, it wouldn't have fallen down, now right? *Right?*"

He smiled.

"So telling that story isn't a slap at the profession, necessarily. It's a story about a bad bridge, and why it failed."

"But what about all the good bridges that don't fall down? Or those amazing feats of engineering?"

"We do those stories, too. They're newsworthy."

"Fair enough. I probably didn't use the best example but you understand where I'm coming from, right?"

"I do. Absolutely. I do. People aren't bridges...or, then again, maybe we are. I dunno."

Their eyes linked while a bond cemented during the lull. Each explained how they needed to get back work. But before leaving, Bradley suggested maybe they could continue their discussion over dinner sometime.

"Sure," she said. "We could do that."

Lunch turned into dinner garnished with a dozen, long-stemmed red roses. More meals followed, enlightened conversation, and at some point, Abby queried:

"You're probably wondering if this is my first time."

"No. Not really," he replied. "But since you raised it, are you experienced?"

Abby had crossed that bridge years earlier, inside a dorm room at Michigan State where she and Michael deciphered the theory of love and the speech of Aristophanes. Michael's father worked at Ford and played saxophone part-time in a local jazz band. Michael was a smooth one and so unlike the other boys she had known in Grand Rapids.

Michael understood that human beings were once whole and round, according to Aristophanes' theory of love. With one head, four ears, and two sets of sexual organs, it was no wonder these extraordinarily strong and mobile creatures might become too ambitious, even arrogant. If mythical gods in Heaven could not understand and respect these humans for who they were, changes would be necessary. That's why Zeus sliced them in half, he said, to assert his control and increase the number of worshippers. It was divide and conquer, he concluded. Zeus sliced us in half, producing our current state, leaving three kinds of human beings: male gender, female gender, and hermaphrodite. Love then, Aristophanes explained, is the quest to be reunited your other half, which also explained homosexuality and heterosexuality. For those sliced from a male sphere would seek love in another male to make themselves whole. Likewise, lesbians were women who had been cut from a female sphere. Ah, but a male or female sliced from a hermaphroditic sphere would seek love in the opposite sex.

Michael surmised that if Aristophanes' theory was correct, then he had undoubtedly been cut from an androgynous being. Abby said she too had been cut from the same such being. She allowed him to seduce her, using Plato's Symposium as his guide. Michael even managed to incorporate a theory of racism into his rap, for which he earned additional style points. For Zeus and the gods, he said, could be interpreted as racist rulers who would try to keep the races divided and prevent them from achieving wholeness as one people.

Yes, Abby agreed. She added Zeus might also be thought of as every girl's father who feared being replaced by the love the daughter felt for another man.

Having reached an understanding of Aristophanes' dinner speech, the two students of philosophy then became one and whole in Abby's dorm room. They used their sexual organs to become one body with one mind, two faces, and four ears. But by the time next semester had rolled around, the class had ended, and she and Michael went their separate ways with passing grades. Meanwhile, Zeus and the other gods could rest easy again.

"So you dig brothers, huh? Is that it?" Bradley smiled broadly. "Goodie."

Her response was an adorable and alluring toothy smile.

Meals turned into drinks at someone's residence. And several drinks led to a kiss. Their very first kiss was timid and restrained. Boy second-guessing girl and vice-versa. It was mechanical, like a vanilla Barbie doll and chocolate Ken trying to hug. The lips of one at first played tag with the lips of the other. Then they stopped, exchanged bashful smiles, and silently agreed: *We're experienced. Let's try it again.*

When their lips connected on the second try, the kiss was soft, wet, and warm. Their bodies were constrained no more. The limbs of chocolate Ken and vanilla Barbie had grown joints.

The first time they made love, Bradley gazed at her face and momentarily wondered if he were hurting her. She had that sensual but sometimes confusing "easy does it" expression. He fought the urge to ask her if everything was okay, and trusted her half-cocked smile was a look of genuine satisfaction.

He could barely contain his excitement and refused to shut his eyes until the very end. He studied the contrasts in their bodies wrapped in that skin. Black on white. White on black. Side by side. Lightness and darkness. Her yin to his yang. Their bodies swirled together like marble. Each color separate and distinct and beautiful on its own, yet even more so together as one finely crafted sculpture of melded black-and-white stone.

In time, he would become arrogant about the way he made love to that woman. He worked hard at perfecting his technique, learning how to be patient, understanding how she moved, and how to touch her. Each time he felt he had turned in a top performance, he smiled to himself with devilish delight.

Abby enjoyed it as well, even though she thought he was a bit too passive the first couple of times. She wasn't a virgin, after all. But she resisted the urge to whisper those words into his ear. Words can be awkward at times. She instead waited patiently for him to relax and to discover her for himself. Once he did so, she responded with affirmation.

Bradley felt whole with Abby. He felt complete. His sometimes-fragile confidence bulked up like a boy who returned to school after summer vacation several inches taller and twenty pounds heavier.

Their love blossomed on the campus of the city's center of culture, along on the grassy embankment surrounding the reflection pool in the front of the planetarium, a half-moon structure that seemed to float on the water like a fisherman's bobber. They studied the names chiseled into in the granite monoliths aligned at the water's edge as though they were archeologists exploring the city's ancient ruins. Suddenly, the names of different city streets and buildings were connected to something real and tangible.

Like children, they dipped and splashed their bare feet in the dirty water, ignoring the signs warning of possible electric shock due to the underwater lighting used to illuminate the fountain on summer evenings.

They wandered the galleries of the art museum, admiring the paintings, sculptures, and other objects by artists they had never heard of. They were among the handful of supporters who dotted the seats in the museum's darkened theatre almost every fall and winter weekend to watch the foreign movies and art-house films, seemingly smuggled into town.

How cleansing and uplifting this urbane space was for them. Abby remarked how it was so unlike the rest of the city, that it almost seemed as if they were in a different city altogether.

Yeah, it was a shame that large swaths of the city were un-acculturated, he said. But that's what made it special—a private sanctuary hidden in plain sight amid a creeping desert of desolation.

Bradley felt right, too, she decided. He didn't sweep her off her feet because that's not the way these things happen. If there was a story to tell of how she knew Bradley was the one—the kind of story that mothers supposedly tell their young, naive daughters as long as it doesn't involve premarital sex, presumably—it would begin with that woman's watch. She saw it on his dresser one night after making love.

The watch looked dated, although it wasn't an antique. Like something one might find at a used clothing store or a flea market. Abby encountered it in a way not unlike the first time she saw that *Colored Only* sign hanging over the toilet in his bathroom. That, too, had stunned her, if only to remind her it really wasn't that long ago. The sign was an antique—at least, that's what the shopkeeper told James when he bought it in Kentucky—and a stunning reminder of the not-so-distant past.

So, too, was that watch. She noticed the watch while placing her earrings on the dresser after returning from the bathroom.

That night, the stars glittered like so many white diamonds tossed upon a blanket of black velvet. The moon was the biggest rock of all. A ray of its light pierced through the venetian blinds and caught just enough of the watch to make it visible in the darkened room. She picked up the watch and caressed it with her thumb and index finger in the moonlight.

The small-face, gold timepiece adorned with golden Roman numerals, and delicate hands kept track of the minutes and hours. It was clearly a woman's watch and its presence troublesome. By this time, there had been enough dinners and drinks to produce a relationship.

She eased back into bed and her white skin vanished underneath the covers as if she were chest deep in murky water. She rested her head on his chest. Her body felt cool against his warm flesh. He instinctively reached for her wrapping his left arm around her torso.

Abby's eyes were open as she pondered that woman's watch. Right there on the dresser in plain view, she couldn't let it pass; her journalistic instincts wouldn't allow it. She had to know. She had dared to stand up to the cold stares and off-handed comments from black women who believed she had stolen one of their few good black men. She ignored remarks from the occasional black man who cooed, Once you go black, you never go back, or something like that. Against the scolding eyes and the remarks of white men who wondered aloud why she would date something like that, she said to hell with them. And to a former friend who told her in one way and another, *I could never date someone of a different race*, Abby replied, *Well, you aren't me, now are you?*

Abby had felt ostracized but stuck by her man because her man had stuck by her. Had it all been a lie and a big waste of time?

"So, is that your girlfriend's watch?" Abby whispered, feigning playfulness in a voice similar to the one she used when asking whether the *Colored Only* sign in the bathroom also applied to her.

"Umm," he grunted.

"The watch on your dresser. Does it belong to that older woman you told me about?" She persisted while the mirth in her voice waned.

"Um-um," he muttered, shifting his head on the pillow. "It's mom's."

Her head popped up like Jack's out of the box. She suddenly felt colder than she did when she had gotten out of bed to pee. The chill ran much deeper.

Remorseful, she apologized on the spot for a tragedy she had nothing to do with as well as for her coldness.

"That's okay," he whispered. "It's not your fault. Is it?" His eyes never opened and the cracked smile and consciousness vanished just like that.

She lay silent.

He had already told her how his mom died in a car crash that she might have survived had she been wearing a seatbelt. But that was well before seatbelt use became routine and the law. It was a time when the restraints were considered excess weight and only got in the way. It was an era when small children moved about as freely inside a moving vehicle as dogs do today.

He was just a little boy then but understood what it all meant. To Abby, he described his memory of his mother as a group of photographs that rest out of sequence in a photo album, some now missing, leaving two-toned pages faded all over except where pictures once lay.

His earliest memory? Her holding him as they waited outside with dozens of other women for Arlan's department store to open for business that day. When Abby asked about its significance, he replied: "I dunno. Her holding me in her arms, I guess."

When he asked her about the earliest memory of her parents, Abby said she could remember sitting in a stroller and her father saying, "Grab my finger."

His fondest memory? That was the time they were playing "the Blob," a name he attached to the game many years later as an adult. He had a blanket over his head as he inched towards his mother, making "monster sounds."

"Mom laid on the couch, crying out for help. I would get close enough to fall over on her. Well, once I was standing too far back from the couch when I started to fall forward. I didn't know it at the time. I landed flat on my face. I guess I looked like a tree falling over, like it had just been chopped down. I was disoriented and didn't know what had happened. But I remember hearing my mother straining to keep from laughing out loud as I stumbled to my feet, trying to get the blanket off of me. I finally get the blanket off and I see her with this pained smirk on her face. She asked if I were all right and said 'Okay, honey, that's enough play for now.' Yeah, I guess that was a couple of years before she died."

Sometime after his mother's death, Bradley asked his father if he could have the watch. He managed to keep it ticking more than two decades years after she had stopped wearing it. But Abby was unaware of that until that night when she spotted the dated timepiece.

She lay on her side with her back to Bradley. He pulled up close behind her and hugged her as if she were a body pillow. She pulled the blanket over his limp arm and her bare shoulders. The two lay together in the stillness of the night.

But she was still awake. Off in the distance, she heard the wail of a siren and the rumble of a freight train.

Inside the room, the only noise was the faint sound of her sniffles. She felt her right eyelash brush against the cotton pillowcase each time she blinked. A tear dripped from her left eye and streamed across the bridge of her nose where it hung. A small, damp circle had formed on the pillowcase just below the corner of her right eye where a tear had been absorbed by the fabric.

Abby wept silently as so many unanswered questions kept her awake until she, too, drifted asleep with Bradley's limp arm wrapped around her body.

That night she dreamt of Socrates and Diotima conversing about the art of love and awakened the next day with knowledge that maybe Bradley was her Diotima. For he had some understanding of absolute beauty, she thought, and maybe he could share some of that wisdom with her.

Those were the nights and days of enchantment. Their love stood out like a bright red toadstool in an aged and shadowy forest, its shade dull and sunlight sparse without their colours.

But after a long stretch of dating and sharing quarters, as well as other concerns, it sometimes seemed as if all tricks had been revealed and the sweet insanity of courtship had curdled.

Inside Lucy's, Bradley stood alone.

The crowd was under the spell of Moses Redmond, as the bluesman channeled Hendrix.

Bradley continued sipping his beer and he entertained the notion of joining the band leader in making a mythical, lyrical escape to Mexico, where they could be free. He then took out a cigarette and struck a match.

Wednesday

So the Bible says and it still is news

9

"Take out a piece of paper, please, and something to write with," Hector Rodriguez commanded.

Abby pushed away her half-eaten bagel and slapped her hands clean before obeying the request.

Day three of diversity training began with roughly half of her forty classmates no longer wearing their nametags. Abby didn't bother pinning hers on that morning either. Nametags created a false sense of familiarity in these types of settings. Readers too often mistakenly believed it eliminated the simple courtesy of personal introductions. She didn't particularly like people she didn't know (men especially) coming up to her, studying her chest, and saying her name—"Well, Abby, what did you think about this morning's session?"

Her table contained a cross section of the conference attendee's occupations. Specialists from human resources took up most of the seats, followed by sales reps and marketing consultants who were there to learn how to talk the talk of their potential customers. A smattering of mid-level managers of some sort or another filled the rest of the seats. Abby, being the lone journalist in the bunch, found some comfort in not being the only woman present. Her table of eight women—one Asian-American, two blacks, and five whites—found plenty of people like themselves. Women were predominant because welcoming and sensitivity issues like diversity often were, without saying, the special province of women and racial minorities, not unlike the job of organizing the department potluck.

Hector was a tall, trim fellow with wavy hair and richly tanned skin that didn't fade once the summer sun set. Abby wasn't alone at her table in noticing his southern hemisphere attractiveness. She heard another woman whisper to a neighbour: "He's fine." But it wasn't much of a whisper. Several other women at the table also heard the remark and smiled as if to say: "Yes, he is."

Observing his exotic handsomeness, his somewhat rumpled appearance, and hearing his Spanish accent, Abby put them all together the instant he took center stage and, in spite of herself, thought about the tango—the dance, not the euphemism for sexual intercourse. She was embarrassed by her quick use of a stereotype; however favourable its connotations might have been for her imaginary dance partner.

Three days earlier, her imagination was seized by a far-less favourable set of ideas when she felt herself surrounded by hordes of Spanish-speaking people after deplaning at Miami International Airport. Maybe it was residual stress from the last few moments of the inbound flight, but she suddenly felt completely isolated and disconnected from those around her. Now there in MIA, she felt overcome by a stifling Third World heat.

The harried pace of people charging through the terminal, dragging bags on wheels, those beeping trucks ferrying others to destinations unknown and the vacant stares in face after face after face unleashed a sense of smallness within her.

She saw plenty of white faces and black faces and bronze faces but felt no relation to any of them. Worse yet, it seemed Spanish was all she heard. She didn't speak Spanish, so she literally had no idea what they were talking about. Why did they talk so fast? She wondered. Were they words of fear and frustration?

Even the public address system broadcast messages and directives were in Spanish. Although the same messages were first delivered in English, she immediately felt excluded once her language barrier had been exposed. And because of it, she felt herself falling into fellowship with xenophobes everywhere if only for that moment.

Abby reminded herself to move as if she knew where she was going. She feigned nonchalance while following the crowd and signs to the baggage claim area. There, she claimed her luggage and began to search for a way out.

The rainy sky made Miami gloomy and depressing, not the south Florida paradise it was supposed to be. A string of taxis sat lined up along the curb like boxcars in a train, waiting to move this human cargo by land. She was directed to hop aboard a car at the front of the line. Even the cabby spoke Spanish as he yelled something out the window and shoehorned the vehicle into traffic.

The experience had left her with a shrinking feeling, a terrible shrinking feeling that she thought she was immune to. She suddenly felt sheltered; a stranger in her own land. She had stepped into a new world and didn't feel a part of it at all, even as a journalist. She feared the world had passed her by, like the friends you once sat around and got drunk with who are now holding down important jobs, traveling, or raising families while you're still hanging out at the same old bar waiting for your life to begin.

How could it be? Hadn't she studied French in high school and fulfilled her foreign language requirement in college? She was preparing to marry someone of a different race. She and Bradley had vacationed together in Montreal where most of the merchants and shop owners greeted their customers in French before switching to English, if necessary. How charming and wonderful and welcoming she thought it was for a non-French speaking visitor. Why did she feel so different now in another bilingual environment?

Abby wanted to retreat to that two-bath, three-bedroom house in that township masquerading as a city.

She wasn't prepared for this marked change in scenery. Perhaps her world had shrunk despite all the promises to herself to never allow that to happen. When she had spoken to Bradley Sunday evening after her arrival, she wasn't so much tired from traveling (although that was part of it), she needed the mental separation to remember she didn't need his hand to walk outside. She had to be alone to remember she was an individual who could take care of herself.

"As a group, Hispanic Americans are difficult to pigeonhole," Hector explained. "We are brown-skinned, light-skinned. We are white.

We are black. But, you see, the term 'Hispanic' does not refer to a racial category. Some of us have Spanish surnames. Some do not. Some of us speak Spanish. And some do not. The cultural influences are European, African, and indigenous, depending upon where you come from—Caribbean, Central America, upper or lower South America."

Hector paused and smiled. He observed looks of subtle confusion to mild irritation on the faces of his pupils.

"On West Coast," he continued, "the word 'Latino' is becoming the preferred umbrella term among Hispanics. You see, the word 'Hispanic' is actually an artificial construction. It was created by the federal government in the early 1970s as a way to classify this disparate population."

Again, he paused. But there were no questions.

"What is your name, sir?" said Hector, to a man seated at a front table.

"Bill," said the man—one of the few white men present.

"And what do you do?"

"I'm director of human resources for a mid-sized manufacturing outfit in Ohio."

"Okay, Bill. Well, I know what you're probably thinking."

He smiled. "And what's that?"

"Bill, here," said Hector, now addressing the entire class, "is probably thinking: 'If Hispanics are indeed such a disparate category of people and difficult pigeonhole, why then bother making any distinctions at all?' Right?"

Bill smiled before yielding a nod and weave, as if to say: *No, that's not what I was thinking. But what the hell? I'll play along.*

Abby, meanwhile, noticed how Hector's 'disparate' sounded like 'desperate.'

The instructor then proceeded to answer the question he'd placed into Bill's mouth:

"There are commonalities. First of all, Hispanics or Latinos, particularly those much less European in their physical characteristics, do face discrimination in housing and jobs and from the police. As with any healthy response to discrimination, we have chosen and are choosing to define ourselves and, in doing so, deciding how we should be addressed. Closely aligned with this idea of choosing one's identity is the right we have to celebrate our unique heritage within the Hispanic diaspora. Now, you hear lots and lots of talk these days from people who say: 'Why can't we simply be Americans?' Well, to that I say, 'We *are* Americans.' That, too, surprises many people because many non-Latinos see us and automatically think 'foreigner' or 'illegal alien.' A lot of that comes from the media."

Abby felt as if all eyes were now upon her.

"Another point I'd like to make is this: Why can't we be *both*? What I mean by that is why can't I be both Latino and American? Eh? Is there anyone in here who's Irish or Italian?"

Several hands went up, including Abby's, whose mother was a descendent of some Irish immigrants who had sailed to America more than 100 years ago. But Abby didn't think often about her strand of Irish ancestry, except maybe on St. Patrick's Day. And even then, it simply provided her with a cute justification to drink green beer with the girls and boys. Besides, she wasn't 100-percent Irish. Her maternal forebears got around, not unlike her father's people. Her father boasted of Norwegian stock, but he also had some French and German blood in his veins. But as she joked with Bradley, Abby said she was basically a mutt, a European mutt.

Nevertheless, she agreed with the speaker's unspoken point about ethnic pride, which was that many white people tended to speak out of both sides of their mouths on the issue of hyphenated Americans. Okay, perhaps they didn't hyphenate their ethnic ancestry. Still, they often spoke proudly of their European roots, or could point to a place on a map where their families had direct ties.

Abby felt compelled to share an experience with her classmates.

"Yes, please," said Hector, enthusiastic for the anecdote and participation.

"I was at a breakfast and seated at a table, like this one here, with eight or nine other people. We were waiting for the program to begin and someone started talking about their European ancestry. Before long, the conversation widened to include most of the table. One man then noted how people from the area had come from all over the place. They mentioned their Scottish heritage, or being Irish, Romanian, Polish, Greek, Italian, whatever."

"Did you participate?" Hector interjected, with his prominent

Spanish accent. "Did you mention your ancestry?"

"Yeah. Yeah. I guess I did."

"And what is that?"

"Well, my people are from all over. My mother is part Irish. My father is Norwegian, German, and French."

"What happened then?"

"Sure. So, anyway, there was this one guy who had assumed something of a moderator's role for the table. I mean, he was sort of leading the conversation. Well, as his eyes moved around the table he suddenly noticed a black woman who was also seated at our table. She hadn't said anything. But when he saw her, he quickly tried to add, or did add, the South to the list of places where people in our area and table had come from. Not Africa or even the Caribbean, for that matter. Just 'the South'; the American South. It seemed really awkward all of a sudden. Kind of forced, like an afterthought."

Abby sensed the stiffening of backs of those present. Stillness swept through the room like the sudden silence in the cabin of an aircraft flying through menacing clouds. She alone controlled the destiny of the gathering at this moment.

"Really. Interesting. So what happened after that? Did you all continue?"

"No. The conversation just sort of died after that. The woman, um, the African-American woman," said Abby, now somewhat reluctant to mention the woman's race, "she just sort of smiled and politely excused herself from the table shortly thereafter, as if to say, 'I'll leave so you guys can talk freely among yourselves.'"

"I see. Interesting. What did you make of that exchange?" Hector queried.

"Well," she teetered. Should she mention her engagement in some fashion? Is now the time? No, she decided. "I guess it showed how we still have trouble in this country talking about our history together whenever race comes into play. From the standpoint of whites, we only want to discuss that part of our history that seems, I don't know, *heroic*, maybe? And when you start talking about how we all arrived here, it becomes awkward for blacks, and whites, too."

Hector nodded deliberatively; he wanted more, it seemed, and for the whole class to hear.

"We don't want to talk about things like slavery during polite table conversation to pass the time. But how could you ignore it when the topic of roots and heritage comes up in such a mixed setting? Now, some whites, like my dad, for instance, will say, 'Well, slavery was a long time ago.' And that's true. It was a long time ago. But it's also true many of the great-grandparents and great-great-grandparents of whites came to this country a long time ago, too. And some came here more recently—earlier in this century. Still, why is it okay to talk about and celebrate that history and yet feel as though the history of blacks is irrelevant or they're dredging up something so uncomfortable for no good reason? I don't know. It just strikes me as a little unfair at times. Well, actually, more than a little. That's all."

Abby now felt self-conscious, noticing the room's undivided and unwanted attention. The time had come to wrap it up.

"So," she concluded, "I could see how an African-American might feel a little excluded and maybe even a little bothered in a situation like that and, the more I think about it, how some whites might feel inclined to keep to themselves, too."

A black woman smiled rather approvingly at her when their eyes met. Abby returned the smile but avoided any further eye contact. To some of her classmates, it seemed as if she had given that speech, or one like it, before. She felt more eyes upon her even after Hector had resumed his program.

"Very good," Hector said. "May I ask what you do for a living?"

"Sure. I'm a reporter."

"Ah, yes," he smiled. "A reporter. You must be one of the good ones."

Hector laughed along with a few of her classmates to push out the cold front that had moved into conference rooms D and E after the unsettling monologue. The speech was a little heavy for an off-site work-related seminar, an otherwise company-funded vacation.

Abby once again had that shrinking feeling.

10

"**A**s-Salaam-Alaikum, brotha."

"Wa-Alaikum-Salaam," he replied.

"All right now!" laughed Curtis, the barber standing behind chair number two; a buzzing set of electric clippers in one hand and a comb in the other. His loud "all right now!" was enough to stall whatever conversation had been going on before Bradley's arrival.

Now, nearly all eyes were on him, the brother sporting the bow tie moving comfortably toward the rear of the narrow storefront, a teetering commercial thoroughfare a few blocks from his childhood home. Warm air blasting from the ceiling-mounted furnace in the back, along with the balminess generated by a space heater in the center of the aisle, added thermal energy to the space. Suspended droplets of oily Soft Sheen sprayed throughout the day to top-off the customers' fresh cuts produced the shop's signature aroma. It smelled like home.

Bradley felt the looks of the few customers present while his image kept pace with him along mirrors that ran the full length of the wall behind the three barber stalls. Bow ties had a way of drawing that kind of attention. On those rare occasions when he wore one, whites and blacks alike were united in their opinion a bow tie warranted some kind of unsolicited commentary. The commentators, however, rarely said "nice tie" and left it at that. No, a bow tie prompted questions of character and authenticity: *Did you tie that yourself or is it one of those clip-on deals? Are you trying to look like an intellectual?*

Then there was the additional question of whether he might be associated with the Nation of Islam. Blacks would simply ask, however jokingly, if he were a Black Muslim.

Whites, on the other hand, could be a little standoffish while eyeing him suspiciously. Even those with whom he had some acquaintance might say: *So, you're wearing a bow tie?* as if to say, *I hope you aren't (or I didn't know) you were one of those black radicals.*

He smiled and nodded hello at the barber in the middle stall, who was busy at work on the head on a youngster. "Hey, pard'ner," said the other barber when their eyes met.

Bradley stopped at the last stall. It had been vacated several months earlier by a young barber who had fled to Atlanta after completing his internship at the shop. Gone from the stall's service counter were the tools of trade present in the other two operating booths. A Clean Ray sanitizer with an assortment of electric clippers aligned underneath the glow of its ultraviolet light like airplanes in a hangar. A square green bottle of Pinaud Clubman Finest Talc, hair spray, Barbicide disinfectant jar, personal effects, and puffy black clouds of clipped 'fro on the floor below also graced the booths. The slate was clean except for an enduring barber styling guide (for black men) poster hanging on the half-wall partition separating the stalls. On the opposite wall, near the 19-inch television, hung a vintage black velvet painting of a soul sister sporting a big Afro, large hoop earrings, and a low-hanging Peace sign medallion shading her pubic region. Bradley shed his overcoat, draped it on a chair nearby, and laid bare the splendor of his neatly tied burgundy-and-navy bow and windowpane shirt. He then slipped into the throne-like barber chair.

"So you down with the Nation these days, huh, bruh?" asked Curtis, following up on his initial greeting.

"Nah. But I'm letting him know that he's on notice," Bradley joked.

"Watch out now!" Curtis bellowed.

Several waiting customers laughed. The second barber merely smiled without looking up.

"What does 'As-Salaam-Alaikum' mean, anyway?" said the customer in Curtis' chair. His tone was earnest, though the question was to no one in particular.

"I dunno," Curtis interjected. "Ask Malcolm X over there."

Picking up on his cue and trying to sound like he hadn't really ever given the greeting much thought, Bradley said: "I think

As-Salaam-Alaikum, means 'peace be unto you.' The reply means—"

"'Right back at 'cha, bruh!',", Curtis interrupted.

The patrons erupted with laughter.

"Yeah, it's something like that." Bradley chuckled. "Actually, it means 'and unto you be peace.'"

After being greeted with *As-Salaam-Alaikum* enough times whenever he wore a bow tie, he finally decided he needed a comeback.

Once the kidding subsided, a customer waiting for his turn in a barber's chair resumed his critique of the Mike Tyson-Buster Douglas fight.

"Man, I'm tellin' you the fight was rigged. Tyson wasn't even throwin' no punches," said the feisty young man who looked to be in his early-twenties.

"He wasn't throwin' no punches because he had this in his face all night—*yah, yah, yah, yah,*" replied Curtis, an experienced 52-year-old, who jabbed his comb-clenched left fist with each "yah."

"Yeah, and he wasn't fakin' when that mouthpiece went flyin' across the ring," said another man.

"There you go."

"Man, boxing is controlled by the Mafia, anyway. Tyson threw that fight 'cause the Mafia told him to," insisted the younger man.

"No he didn't," said Curtis.

"Yes he did. Rocky Marmalano, Marma—, Mar— whatever the hell his name is. You know who I'm talkin' about, tho."

The other barber glanced up when he heard the word "hell."

Bradley chuckled with delight at the amusing exchange.

"Marciano," said Ellis Cunningham, the barber in the middle stall. He didn't look up from the boy's hair he was working on. "Be still boy," he said, to the squirming four-year-old.

His mother, who sat nearby, said to her son, "Be still for Mr. Ellis, Brandon."

"Yeah, that Italian white boy. The Mafia didn't want to see his undefeated record broken, 'specially by no brotha. And you know the Mafia ain't nothin' but Italians. And Italians don't like black people. Am I right?"

There was no answer.

"Don't y'all remember that scene from *The Godfather*," he

continued, "when those Mafia dudes decided to sell the dope in the black neighbourhoods?"

"Yeah, all right, bruh," laughed Curtis, as he nudged his customer on the shoulder.

"That's the same way they did Larry Holmes when he lost to Spinks the first time."

"See, now, I ain't gonna argue with you about that Spinks-Holmes fight, cause I just happenin' to agree with you," Curtis chuckled. "But Tyson? I ain't buying it. That brotha just got his butt whupped that night. Where was that fight, anyway? Japan, wasn't it?"

"Yeah, I think so," said someone.

"Shoot, Mafia ain't got no business in Japan. Those little Japanese people got they own Mafia to worry about. Shoot. Besides, they too busy making Walkmans for y'all little Negroes over here to run out and spend all y'all hard-earned money on." Curtis chuckled at himself.

Ellis smiled.

"Eh, man?" said the talkative customer, changing the subject. "What do y'all make of that shootin' the other day?"

Bradley looked up but had no desire to engage in a barbershop debate. He had seen that type enough times in the barbershop to know you couldn't win arguments with guys like that. It was best to just let them talk themselves out, not unlike the way an undisciplined boxer keeps throwing punches at the air. That is, of course, unless you were someone like Curtis Terry who was skilled at brushing aside opposing arguments by sheer force of wit. And then there was the way of Ellis. But this topic was different.

"What's to make of it?" Ellis asked.

"You think they should charge that man?"

"If the man broke the law, he broke the law," said Curtis. "Ain't that right, El?"

"If the shoe fits."

"See, I disagree. I disagree. See, this wouldn't be an issue if that was a white man who did what that brotha did in shooting at those gang-bangers."

"*What?*" Curtis exclaimed. "Man, y'all hear that? Boy, don't 'cha know the N-double-A-C-P woulda been all over that? Yeah, and I woulda been right there with 'em." He laughed and the barbershop erupted once again. "Shoot."

"You don't think he crossed the line when he started shooting up the street?" said Ellis.

"Eh, he was just protectin' hisself and his family and his property."

"*Protectin' hisself?*"

"Yeah. That's the way I see it."

"Yeah, all right, John Wayne," Curtis laughed. "We gonna start callin' you The Duke. Of course, you do know that The Duke is make-believe, too, right?"

"Naw, man, don't call me John Wayne. Cause dude was a redneck, too." He laughed and turned to get a fist bump from a neighbour.

"I wouldn't be surprised if the prosecutor doesn't charge him," said C.T.'s customer. "Man, the way black folks came out and supported him last time he ran? And he's up for re-election next year, too?"

"Yeah, you got a point," said C.T.

"So why not cut a hard-working black man some slack, especially if they catch those dudes who stuck him up? *Psssh*. Besides, white folks probably couldn't care less."

"*Word.*" The feisty young customer jumped in. "Cause it's not their neighbourhood, so what do they care about some niggas shootin' up their own block?

"Not in here, sir."

"Yeah, niggas be like: *pap-pap-pap*." He gestured with his gun-shaped hand drawn, firing imaginary bullets.

"Hey? *Hey?* We aren't having that in here. Okay?" said Ellis, his tone a silencer. He also motioned toward the youngster in his chair. "We straight, pard'ner?"

"Oh, my fault, my fault," he said, lowering his hand. "But y'all know what I'm sayin'. Y'all know what I'm sayin', tho."

"Oh yeah, I hear what you're saying. That nobody really cares about nothing. And that's the problem," said Ellis, as his eyes drilled a hole into the fake gunman. "See what *I'm saying?*"

The young man smiled and nodded slightly. "Yes, sir, I do."

"Not only that," said Bradley, who chimed in with princely certainty, "but the deed was done. Right?"

The shop went silent except for the sound of hair being cut

and hot air escaping the furnace. The adult eyes in the shop again shifted in Bradley's direction, including those of the two barbers. Little Brandon, however, remained focused on getting out of that big, ol' barber's chair as soon as possible.

"So, this guy is going to risk killing or wounding them, or a neighbour, or a child, over a Walkman," Bradley continued, "all because he *snapped*?"

His prosecutorial rebuke sealed the debate.

"Preach, young Malcolm!" C.T. exclaimed.

All present—Brandon excluded—then laughed. Case closed.

Ellis proceeded to unfasten the smock draped around the little boy, much to the youngster's relief. With his whiskbroom, he brushed away the loose hair from his shoulders and torso. "All right young man."

The boy wasted no time climbing down from that great, big barber's chair. His mother gave him twelve dollars to give to the barber. She then told her son to tell the barber to keep the change. The shy little boy followed his mom's directions without a hitch.

"Thank you, Mr. Brandon," the barber said to his little customer. Ellis extended his hand for Brandon to shake. Again, the little guy followed along. The handshake began as a traditional handshake that flowed naturally into a soul brother's grip between the four-year-old boy and the man old enough to be his granddaddy. "You be cool now. Alright?"

The bashful little boy nodded.

"Thanks, Ellis," said the boy's mother as they began move towards the exit.

"Thank you, Mrs. Watson. We'll see y'all again next time. Okay, pard'ner?"

Brandon nodded yes quickly but avoided eye contact.

"Okay, B, show time," said his father.

"Eh, I think I'm next," said the feisty customer, who seemed to think vigilantism had a place in contemporary America.

"I'm sorry, sir. This gentleman here has a standing appointment with me. See his name is right here on the list. But your turn is coming and it won't be long."

"Oh, my fault. My fault. Not tryin' to take cuts or nothin', no pun intended. Ha. Ha," said the customer, who sat down again and resumed his side conversation with his neighbour. "Yeah, dawg, so anyway like I was sayin'…."

Bradley sat down in the barber's chair and his father wrapped him in his barber's cape. Before fastening it behind his neck, he wrapped tissue paper around Bradley's neck to keep the freshly chopped hair from seeping past his collar and down into the shirt.

His father started right into the job. Using the electric clippers, he worked from the bottom up along the sides and back of Bradley's head. The barber clipped a little and then used his comb to smooth a section of hair down into place again.

"Talk to me, son." his father said. "How're things?"

Bradley shared his frustration about how the installation project at work was dragging and how management had begun to get antsy. "I swear sometimes it seems like it takes our trades people forever to do a job. And if you so much as look at an electric panel, the electricians will stop their *break* and threaten to walk out."

Dad laughed.

"Well, you know the first three words that shopworkers learn, don't you?" said Curtis, who had been eavesdropping and realized he might be missing something after he heard laughter: "Call ma' committeeman!"

There were several chuckles throughout before the son and father resumed chatting.

"Then it seems like there's always a dumb redneck lurking about."

"Mm-hmm."

Ellis never worked in the shop, unlike many of his friends and customers. For him, it was an oppressive place. He grew up watching his daddy come home day after day broken down and exhausted from the heat of the Buick foundry. The work was filthy, back-breaking, and dangerous. But it was one of the few jobs blacks could get in the shop when his father arrived here from Georgia in 1921. The only other jobs were in plant sanitation.

Even then, it could still be difficult for black men to get in the door. His father, Ernest, born at the turn of the century in Georgia, was nicknamed "Sam" because of an experience he had with a hiring clerk at Buick years ago during the great migration. When he went to apply for a job, the white man looked at him and said:

"What's your name? *Sam*?"

"*Yeah*!" replied an angry Ernest.

So, that's how Ernest Cunningham came to be known as Sam among his family and co-workers. It was their little inside joke.

Ellis told his sons about passing by the in the summertime and seeing the guys all laid out on the yard, probably on the edge of heat exhaustion without even knowing it. The job had black written all over it, Ellis concluded, and it's why he never wanted to work in the shop. He didn't want to be constantly reminded it was the only job he could get in the factory. He didn't want to be reminded of anything negative connected with being black.

That's why he hated to see or read about some black person *fuckin' up*, although Ellis generally avoided the use of such profanity. He even frowned on it in his barbershop and would tell a customer to watch his mouth if his language became too foul. But in his private thoughts, only *fuck* captured the depths of his anger and frustration. Few things upset him more than black folks *fuckin' up*. Not because blacks are supposed to be perfect, he said, but because white folks think that we are. Before we were less than human, he said, now we're supposed to be superhuman. No, it wasn't fair. But he knew the score and wanted his boys to know it as well.

Though he never stepped foot in a factory, he seemed especially proud of Bradley. Equipped with an engineering degree, Bradley had entered the place on his terms, Ellis believed. That was key. It paid well and the benefits were good. And if that's what his son wanted to do, well, he was all for it.

Ellis liked cutting hair and enjoyed the barbershop camaraderie. He built his shop into a fine establishment on the city's southside. It took many long hours of standing on his feet, listening to a lot of shit-talkers, and an occasional burglary; but he did it. Although his prices were a little higher than other shops, his many loyal customers didn't seem to mind too much. His barbers all wore matching smocks, and his shop was a training ground for many apprentice barbers through the years. He even sponsored a Little League team for the neighbourhood boys some years ago. He wanted a professional operation where people could relax and trust him to be there.

He also needed the stability because he had two boys to raise. It wasn't unheard of for Ellis to open the shop at eight in the morning and be there until after midnight. Because he often worked long, sometimes irregular hours, Bradley and his brother, James, spent plenty of time at grandma and grandpa's house.

Ellis never dated much during those years, and the boys recalled very few women coming by the house to visit their father. Years later, they learned that daddy sometimes took extended lunch or dinner breaks to make house calls on lady friends. When Bradley asked once why he hadn't remarried while his boys were growing up, dad was matter-of-fact:

"What do you say to a woman when you've got two small boys? 'Would you like to get married and raise my sons for me?' What woman really wants to do that? A woman wants to care for her own babies. I already had two and wasn't looking to add on."

When he did remarry a few years after James graduated from high school, Bradley was initially, though quietly, resentful of his father's new bride. He was jealous. Sure, he could relax somewhat now that his children had completed high school. But Bradley had heard stories about how the old man was a little more fun before mom was killed. He was looser; more relaxed. His mother's early death transformed his father into someone more cautious and serious. Almost overnight, he went from being a daddy who roused his boys from bed in the morning singing the chorus from James Brown's hit, *Get Up*; to a father who taught his sons how to use an alarm clock.

Bradley had hoped to see the father of his early youth resurrected in some way, and to be a part of it, once he had been relieved of the pressure of raising two boys alone.

What exactly they would have done together, he had no idea really. They didn't hunt or fish. But when Freda emerged from the background and became Ellis' wife, Bradley felt as if she were stealing precious time from him. Bradley also felt that maybe his father had been avoiding James and him during their formative years, and simply used the demands of his barber's job as a convenient excuse.

Ironically, Bradley thought about calling Freda "mama" once his maturity was restored. The boys wanted so much to have a mother to buy a Mother's Day present for. Bradley thought it would be quaint to call Freda "mama," even though she had grown children of her own from a previous marriage. Calling her by her first name seemed not quite respectful enough. Not that it was disrespectful. But the first-name basis didn't seem to put her on par with her mate—his father. Calling her "Mrs. Cunningham" seemed awkward, stilted, and cold. So for a long time he simply addressed her carefully without the use of any names or titles. But that too seemed to be a denial of her existence and a cop out.

Eventually, he settled on calling his father's wife Freda. She didn't seem to mind at all being called by her name.

They didn't often talk about Abby. Ellis didn't approve of their living arrangements and said so. It was so uncharacteristic of his son's otherwise deliberate approach to life. After being told Abby was now sharing Bradley's house in Grand Heights, the father cut to the chase: "So whose stuff is it really?"

The son replied, half-jokingly, that it was still his house and Abby only lived there. "Besides, she still has her own place."

Joking or not, Ellis was unconvinced. "Oh, I see," he said. "One foot in, one foot out. So y'all don't really live together, huh?"

Bradley wondered whether his father's disapproval of their living arrangement was simply another one of his convenient excuses. He suspected his father was equally troubled, if not more so, of his interracial courtship.

That was the word, according to James, who had said, "Daddy-O says he'll be happy when you get over your white-girl thang once and for all."

Unmoved, Bradley pushed back against his brother's unsolicited perspective: "Are you speaking for dad now…or yourself?"

Hard to know if dad actually said that or if James was simply being James, Bradley concluded. But he knew his father thought the city, and country for that matter, still very much had problems with matters of race. He said on more than one occasion in the barbershop how white folks loved to play the blame game. Just look at all those fiascoes downtown, he said. All of them were ill-conceived, pie-in-the-sky nonsense. And one day, he just went off:

"All these factories start closing up and all those easy-money jobs start drying up. Now the city's broke and going to hell. Whose fault is it? Black folks. When open housing came, man, there wasn't no open housing. Hell no. White folks split, Jack. And that was that. Oh yeah, now, we black folks can be something else, too. But to hear these white folks tell it, they didn't have nothing whatsoever do with the state of things. And that's some bull."

His father's tirade was rather surprising because he'd generally kept his frustrations to himself. He rarely used his boys to vent. How could he? What could they possibly do with that kind of information? Recognizing and avoiding direct threats to your immediate, personal safety is one thing; subjective threats require a different kind defense, however. So he simply tried to make sure they were prepared.

On the topic of Bradley's romantic choices, he'd told Freda that even though he was less than enthusiastic about his son crossing the colour line, a part of him wanted to believe couples like that were okay; that they really were no different than other relationships.

"I remember the first time you brought home one of your little white gals," he told Bradley sometime later after Bradley announced his engagement. "I thought: '*What is this little Negro trying to do? Why does he want to hurt himself like that? What would his mother say?*' I even thought that maybe I hadn't brought enough black women around for you to see."

Bradley remembered that day as well; the first time he brought a white girl home. He was a college freshman at the time, and it was a Sunday afternoon. His father was sitting in the living room with Aunt Josephine when Bradley walked through the door with this white girl. His father stood up, greeted the pair, and promptly excused himself from the room. Even Bradley misread the reaction. He thought his father was being polite and giving the two a little privacy. Aunt Josephine also left the room a short time later so her brother's exit wouldn't look so clumsy.

But when Bradley went into the kitchen to get himself and the girl a pop, he saw a tormented man leaning against the counter and frowning at the floor. His father couldn't even look him in the eye.

Over time, things began to change.

"So you say Abby's in Miami?" said the father, resuming their conversation after a brief lull.

"Yeah," said Bradley, surprised by the query. "There since Sunday. She'll be back on Friday."

"And you didn't want to go?"

"Couldn't afford the time off right now."

"Uh-huh. So you get to be a bachelor for real again this week, huh?"

The two men laughed.

"Well, good. Enjoy it while it lasts."

"Yeah."

"Still no date yet?"

"Nope. We're still talking about late summer, early autumn. I guess we need to make a decision fairly soon before everything starts filling up." He sighed.

"Well, like I said, enjoy this time while it lasts. 'Cause when it's over."

They chuckled a little more.

"Eh, El," Curtis said, "you and young Malcolm over there been having too much fun this afternoon."

"All right now, C.T., remember who you're dealing with. And why don't you mind your own business for a change, anyway?"

"If that's Malcolm in your chair, then you must be the Honorable Elijah Muhammad, since you the daddy and all."

"C.T., man, lay off the pipe. Alright?" Ellis shot back.

The barbershop was again alive with laughter.

"Awww," Curtis chuckled. "See. Why you gotta go there?"

11

Daniel Yang stood docile before the room of chattering adults. He said nothing for what seemed like a long time and stared at a spot on the back wall. The group, having just returned from lunch and still rather jumpy, was slow to catch on. However, Mr. Yang's unspoken patience and orderly demeanor finally lulled them into obedience. They quieted themselves and yielded the floor to the slender man dressed in a black suit.

"Asian-Americans," Mr. Yang began, his voice light and airy; his words enunciated carefully, "are often called a 'model *mi-nor-i-tee*.' A model *mi-nor-i-tee*. You should ask yourselves: A model *mi-nor-i-tee* compared to what? African-Americans? Latinos, perhaps? Be wary of this description. Do not fall victim to this kind of stereotyping."

He stopped and looked out over his audience, most of whom now felt a strange vibe emanating from Mr. Yang. He left his post behind the lectern and began to stroll the room, hands clasped behind his back.

"Confucius told of how Tsze-kung once asked the Master, 'Is there one word which may serve as a rule of practice for all one's life?' The Master replied, 'Is not *444* such a word? What you do not want done to yourself, do not do to others.'"

Mr. Yang held the room's undivided attention.

"Confucius also say, 'The beginning of wisdom is to call things by their proper names.' And so with that in mind, ask yourselves this: If Asian-Americans are the model *mi-nor-i-tee* and so damn smart, then why don't you see more of us in management?"

The remark prompted a few restrained snickers in the back of the room. Abby observed a difficult smile on the face of her lone Asian-American classmate, a woman of Japanese descent whose grandparents, she later learned, had spent time in an internment camp during World War II.

Daniel Yang, executive director of the Asian-American Institute, then stopped at table of six people near the front of the room. He observed the group momentarily before reaching into his jacket's inside pocket. He pulled out a small camera and snapped a quick photograph of the people seated there.

"What's an Asian in America without a camera, right?" said Daniel, in a different and far less ethnic sounding voice.

The class erupted with laughter.

"Okay," he confessed, amid the laughter, "I guess it's usually Japanese businessmen you see toting cameras. But same difference, right?"

Walter Montgomery and Anne Riley were delighted the group had been had by their presenter's little skit.

After the group quieted down, Daniel, who had done some theatre years ago in college and insisted everyone call him by his first name, said, "Let me ask this: How many of you expected to hear a gong resonate when I walked into the room? C'mon, you can be honest. That's what we're here for."

The comment drew more laughs though not as many as the previous outburst.

"I do want to talk a bit about the myth of the 'model minority.' I say myth because that's exactly what it is," said Daniel, straight-faced and moving about more freely. "Be wary of the speaker who invokes this description when talking about Asian-Americans for a couple of reasons. First, I see it as a divide-and-conquer tactic to build tension between minority groups. During my introduction, which was meant to be comical, by the way, I alluded to this. I tried to use a little humor because it helps alleviate the underlying tension that's usually present in these discussions. But, anyway, does anyone know what I'm talking about with this divide-and-conquer strategy?"

"Yes," said a white woman. "I believe it's when you raised the question whether Asians were a model worth emulating for blacks and Hispanics."

"Right. Now don't misunderstand," he said, pausing to scan the room. "I think different groups can and should learn something from other groups. In fact, I believe it's imperative we develop a deep affection and respect for one another as people. That's the reason we're here, right? But my point is that Asian-Americans tend to be portrayed today as the impossibly good or perfect or intelligent minority. And usually it's done as a way to undermine affirmative action, which I support, by the way, or other social programs. 'Hey, the Asians can do it, what's your problem, black man?'"

The bluntness of his last remark stunned.

"I also believe there's something else at work. Basically, what the person is saying is for African-Americans and Latinos to sit down, and shut up, and try being like that model student over there we never hear a peep out of. So it's a way to assuage white guilt. Sure, education is very important in many Asian-American households. That's nothing to be ashamed of. But if you believe some people, we have taken over higher education in some quarters. Incidentally, does anyone know what UCLA stands for?"

Abby considered raising her hand.

Before anyone could offer an answer, Daniel gave it.

"United Caucasians Lost among Asians. Get it? We'll discuss more on that later. Right now, I want to continue with this image of the model student, or the model minority that we're made out to be. The model student is nice, obedient, doesn't cause problems, and gets all As. In some cases they're picked on, right? Meanwhile, African-Americans and Latinos are typically thought to be loud or more boisterous; people more likely to speak out if they've been wronged, right? Someone who'll punch you in the nose…And, of course, like our Hispanic brothers and sisters, we're all thought to be recent immigrants. I cannot tell you the number of times that I've been asked how long I've been in this country or been complimented on my English. Once at an airport," he chuckled, "I complimented a guy who had been talking about his German ancestry on how well he spoke English."

The class chuckled.

"…But that's another story. This myth of the model minority also suggests that America has welcomed Asians with open arms. Well, allow me to share with you this afternoon a *few ancient Chinese secrets,*" said Daniel, resurrecting his earlier Chinese accent. His didacticism, however, seemed to have deadened his comedic appeal for some. He reviewed some 140 years of U.S. immigration history before stopping at Angel Island.

"Anyone here ever hear of Angel Island?"

Two hands went up.

"Anyone else?"

A model minority. The description also had resonance for Abby. Was Daniel correct in surmising that the portrayal of Asian-Americans as America's perfect houseguests as a not-so-subtle swipe at blacks? Absolutely.

In view of certain family members (notably her father), Bradley could have been any other race and it would have been okay, she thought. Not ideal, but okay.

In her father's view, blacks were different, though not exotic. They stood out too much. Yet it wasn't a matter of language that set them apart. No, it was something else. Blacks seemingly had an indefinable quality of separateness. Perhaps it was their skin colour and kinky hair. Maybe it was because they had no native place to call their own, like wandering children longing for their motherland.

Whatever it was, Dennis Larsen really couldn't understand what his daughter saw in that black man. He and Bradley were certainly nothing alike, he thought, except they were both men with love for Abby. Nor would life get any easier for her by marrying him. "This world already has enough problems," he counseled. "Why add this one to the mix?" You can do badly by yourself, he concluded.

Dennis more or less treated his black customers no differently than any others, and even disallowed the use of the word "nigger" in his home. But this same man regarded his daughter's pending interracial marriage as something akin to a rich girl foregoing her inheritance and marrying beneath her. It didn't matter to him that Abby's only inheritance was her white skin. That, and maybe the shoe store he owned. But that was beside the point.

He focused instead on the future grandchildren. No doubt they would be black even if they looked white. They would be black and forever marked with that indefinable quality of separateness. And if they came out with permanently browned skin, which was quite likely because of Bradley's complexion, there could be no faking it for the white grandparents pushing the stroller in the park.

Could he love such a grandchild in the same way? Love; meaning would he be able to see himself in his daughter's offspring, and give to them what his grandfather had given to him? Would they be his grandchildren or *theirs*? He wondered.

Her father was one of those men of his generation lucky enough to experience some kind of survivor's guilt. Vietnam got hot a bit after his time had passed, which, Abby concluded, caused him to undergo a period of self-examination on what he might have done if called upon to serve.

To make matters worse, he had grown up with a guy whose kid brother was still listed as missing in action somewhere in Southeast Asia. To honor his memory of the neighbourhood boy, Dennis sported an MIA sticker on his car's bumper, which caused Bradley to remark to Abby once: "You should tell him that he's not coming back." A mean thing to say, she thought at the time.

It seemed her father spent countless hours watching television documentaries on the war of his generation, analyzing it as if the outcome could have been altered somehow. Her grandfather was awarded a Purple Heart during World War II after taking shrapnel while serving somewhere in Italy.

Abby suspected her father wondered privately whether he measured up to that man, but not enough to enlist in the service. Perhaps it was easier and less complicated to imagine it instead. His grandfather didn't volunteer for war; he was drafted.

Since his number wasn't called, Dennis spent the Sixties at home watching the civil rights movement unfold on the flickering, sometimes snowy, screen of a black-and-white television set. He felt sorry for the black marchers and protesters, and even entertained the idea of participating himself in some fashion. But there were some things a young, married father must pass on if it isn't necessary or central to one's primary responsibilities. So he avoided active participation in those historic events, observing from afar as other young whites demonstrated alongside blacks. The so-called sexual revolution passed him by, too.

He could identify with the mission to stop the madness in the South. He lived vicariously through them all the way until the faint cries of *Black Power!* began wafting North. While it may have satisfied a longing for some sort of empowerment, those words, joined together—that phrase—added an 'ir' to *the* struggle, turning it into *their* struggle. Put off by the fiery rhetoric he heard, he wondered if any white person had a place in this proposed country ruled by *Black Power!* So he stopped paying attention to *their* cause and concentrated on his business of fixing and selling shoes for walking and running. And in his own way, Dennis helped to ensure he wouldn't have to worry about whether he'd ever have a place in a country ruled by black power.

Then his only daughter became smitten with a black guy. But hell, it was more than that now. They were engaged.

Abby and Bradley were leaning toward a small, private affair for family members and a few close friends. Initially, they talked about something large and expensive. Now they thought a modest gathering would be more intimate, personal, and romantic instead of some conspicuous, overdone celebration—as if King's dream had been realized.

Privately, the idea of seeing a church with all the black people seated on one side and white people on the other was too much to think about on what was supposed to be the happiest day of their lives. Granted, seating based upon whether a guest was closest to the bride or groom was traditional and expected. But skin-colour contrasts always seemed to complicate these otherwise trivial distinctions.

Abby's mom wasn't exactly thrilled by her daughter's decision to marry outside of the race either. But unlike her ex-husband, she didn't see it as the end of all things. Everyone would keep his or her comfortable distance and that would be that. Besides, she said, Abby would discover soon enough that all men were created equal.

When her father finally met Bradley, Abby recalled the two men shook hands like the heads of two states—one vanquished, the other victorious.

Dennis was more or less pleasant, not unlike the way he treated his black customers at the store. Still, Dennis looked as though he had to swallow hard as he prepared to hand over property loss as part of some brokered peace accord.

Abby's mind drifted back into the present as Daniel Yang shared a few more stories about the indignities that took place on Angel Island.

The speaker then made another observation.

"If this is how America treated members of its model-minority class, what did it save for members of the other groups who weren't as fortunate as those of us of Asian descent?"

12

Bradley phoned Abby at the Miami Hyatt Regency where she'd checked in for the week but there was no answer. They hadn't spoken since yesterday afternoon, closing the call on a rift that had spider-webbed quickly like a sheet of thin ice fracturing under a great weight.

Bradley had held fast to his position. Despite her curiosities and sincerity to compensate for her naivete, he fumed. She couldn't understand what it really meant to be a man, a black man like him. *A brotha*. No matter how much stupid diversity training she signed onto, the nuances would forever elude her grasp. Their quarrel was about a news story that had nothing to do with them. But in Bradley's mind, it had everything to do with how the world saw them—a black man and a white woman each enthralled by intimacy; engaged to wed the following year. And maybe, just maybe, he wasn't ready for it after all. Maybe he'd had enough.

After hanging up, he'd lingered for a while in the dark shadows of their empty house looking out the windows from different views; a front window here, a rear window there. He watched a black-and-white tabby cat tiptoe across his backyard before vanishing into a thicket of shrubbery.

Earlier that night, Bradley walked out of the too-warm Red Lobster alone. The cold night air felt like a face slap. As soon as he got in the car, he slid Jimi Hendrix into the cassette player.

...When I'm sad she comes to me
With a thousand smiles she gives to me free
It's alright she says...it's alright
Take anything you want from me
Anything...

Fuck. Jimi's voice, riding shotgun, magnified his loneliness and Bradley found himself driving across town to The Cabaret. He traveled free of the anxiety that his little diversion might be discovered later by Abby, who called strip clubs a gateway drug for the attached. An anachronism. "Why would you ever think about turning back the clock?" she had asked. To which he thought: *Maybe some things never really go out of style.*

Settling himself at a bistro table, he watched as a waitress closed in with laser-like accuracy. Her black hot pants, tuxedo halter top, and bow tie gave the boys' club a formal air. The Cabaret wasn't some low budget tits-and-ass joint next to a junkyard or across the street from some old, rusty factory. This titty bar was a gentleman's club that featured a daily businessman's lunch special.

The waitress lowered a clean ashtray on top of the butt-and-ash-filled dish on his table and removed them both with a slight-of-hand maneuver. Placing the fresh ashtray on the table, she asked, "What can I get you, sir?"

"Bud Light, please."

"Coming right up."

He pulled out a cigarette, lit up, and checked out the club's shadowy interior as he unbundled himself. The scene was the same as always. The DJ roosted in his pulpit to the right of the stage, his face ghostly in the darkened room amid wafting cigarette smoke and muted red light radiating from the turntable. The spell he cast was some head-banger tune from the strip-joint's greatest hits collection.

Bradley slipped the waitress an extra dollar once she returned with his longneck brew.

The night was slow.

The T-shaped stage, glowing beneath a kaleidoscope of red, blue, yellow, and green light was empty except for two erect brass poles posted along the short runway. The parallel props served no structural purpose, just a pair of toys waiting for a dancer. The main stage's back wall—floor to ceiling mirrored glass—created a spacious illusion.

A few of the scantily clad dancers milled about like subway pickpockets waiting for the next money train to arrive. Two or three women, however, had already found wallets to latch onto. At individual tables, these ladies moved like giant wind-up dolls, grinding away slowly between the legs of their eager boys.

The song ended and the stage show resumed with the uncorked energy of Guns N' Roses' *Paradise City.*

Bradley sat through a couple of performances as the dancers were routed on and off the elevated stage with the efficiency of an automated assembly line. All the while, he drained two beers and burned another cigarette.

He declined an offer for a table dance from a roaming stripper who had begun working the room as if she were carrying a tray of hors d'oeuvres. Not finding a buyer in Bradley, she proceeded to the next table where a single guy invited her to have a seat.

"Next up is Luscious," said the ghost face with the spooky DJ's voice.

The lean dancer marched on stage in harmony with J. Geils Band *Centerfold*, a song whose harmonica lead-in and chorus of *Na-na-na-na-na-na-na-na-na* always reminded Bradley of Civil War-era music.

Not merely the same old, same old, Bradley took note of the difference immediately. "Oh, a sista," he muttered to himself.

She was pleasingly fudge-complexioned, her silky straightened black hair pulled back into ponytail. A wig, for sure. But so what, he thought. Her gear was athletic—white Spandex hot pants and matching cropped tank top that reminded Bradley of a harness. The shirt's bottom skirted just below her areolas. Her shoes were the standard dance footwear—platform stilettos. But they glittered like Dorothy's.

Luscious danced with powerful grace immediately out of the gate. Her motions were fluid, if not particularly sensual. She was a thoroughbred among erotic hoofers. This woman was born to dance, he thought. And he imagined nothing would be different, even if an audience wasn't present. She could have danced all by herself. Bradley decided right then that she was the one. She merited a stage visit. He readied a bill as she ascended the runway to the main staging area.

For the second of her two-song set, Luscious was unharnessed. The top and hot pants had come off, and the DJ slowed the music to Prince's *Do Me, Baby*; words Bradley had playfully crooned to Abby from time to time.

Bradley watched his game move across the stage with an exaggerated yet controlled gait. Her legs crossed over the other as if she were toying with a police officer during a field sobriety test. The dancer made her way to the first of the two brass poles and stopped with her back to it. She then slid down the pole slowly as if she were melting. With her back against the pole, she came to rest on her hams. Her elevated heels sharpened the definition of her slender calves.

Bradley took another sip of courage before standing up. He moved casually towards the woman, eyes transfixed by hers, under her spell.

Standing at the stage's edge, he sheepishly shot a glance or two at her crotch. He avoided himself in the mirror and instead focused on the reverse image of the woman's ass as she continued to face him. In his fingers he held a folded ten-dollar bill.

Luscious lunged forward from the squatting position onto all fours. The dancer crawled in rhythm to the money peeking between his fingers. She smiled. Bradley smiled. And the distance between them narrowed with the pace of the slow jam.

Upon meeting Bradley at the edge of the stage, she rolled over onto her back then sat up with her legs elevated, extended like outstretched arms. Her physicality was impressive—her tightened, flat abs an inviting pan of sliced, moist brownies—and Bradley allowed his eyes to travel the contours of her body before stopping at her eyes.

"How are you doing handsome?"

"Fine. I'm definitely digging your performance. You're the best dancer here." Bradley, intoxicated by the freedom of the moment, felt his pants beginning to push away from his crotch, thoughts of Abby set aside.

She held the smile and spread-eagle position but said nothing until Bradley inserted the ten spot into the ruffled garter that bandaged her upper thigh.

"Oh, thank you, baby."

She winked at him as Bradley held his chicken grin. The dancer rolled onto her stomach and proceeded to pump the floor with a slow, rhythmic pulse.

Bradley maintained his close-up view a moment longer before retreating to his table for a drink and smoke. Luscious wandered over a short time later to thank him for his generous tip.

"Would you like some company?" she asked.

Of course, he said, and followed up by offering to buy her a drink.

Bradley lit up another Marlboro Light as Luscious retrieved a box of Virginia Slims from her tiny purse filled with a wad of bills.

"Thank you." She mumbled, leaning closer to the flickering lighter in his hand, cigarette pressed between her purple-stained lips.

Over drinks and smokes, he moved to shift their chance meeting beyond the impersonality of a business transaction, first praising her dance skills before asking how much a dancer could make in a place like this.

Luscious looked at him sideways as she blew out smoke from the corner of her mouth, away from his face.

"I'm not a cop or anything. I'm not from the IRS," he explained. "I'm just curious. I mean, you don't have say how much you make."

"You can do all right…if you're good. It's not unheard of for a dancer to make a thousand dollars or more in a week's time."

"*Really?*"

Yes, she nodded. "I generally work five nights a week. You figure with tips and table dances and couch dances, it adds up. Then you have your regulars. Like I have this one guy that's been coming to see me, a white man who's a bank vice president or something like that. He comes in every week and gives me three hundred dollars."

"Three hundred?"

Yeah, she nodded through a cloud of smoke.

"So what do you give these guys in return?"

"Umm, companionship. You know, I give him a certain number of table or couch dances. Sit there and just talk to him. He tells me about his job or his wife and things."

"All that for three bills?" He chuckled. "So, what is that? Your platinum package or something?"

"Mm?"

"Nothing." He smiled. "Just making a joke."

"Oh, yeah, well, I have other regulars too," she boasted. "But he's the only one that pays me that much."

"So how does someone get to be a regular?"

"It takes time. Mostly, they'll come in and ask for the same girl night after night. They're usually big tippers…They also tend to be married." She took a drag from the cigarette as she checked him out.

Bradley paused and wondered who was sizing up whom. He puffed his cigarette and asked, "Let me ask you something: Do you ever get aroused while dancing? I mean, while you're working."

"You mean sexually?"

"Yes."

"Hmm. Sometimes…But not often."

Luscious was expressionless as she continued with her private groove while smoking the hell out of that Virginia Slim. She looked at Bradley quizzically for a moment, as though she felt his eyes upon her. Luscious blew out another plume of smoke then rubbed her knee lightly against his outer thigh.

"Let me ask you something." Her voice mildly seductive as she grazed an index and middle finger underneath his jawline before sliding off his lightly stubbled chin. The hint of perfume, just a touch, was mesmerizing compared to the soap-and-water freshness of Abby. She smiled. "How often do you get aroused? At work, I mean."

The question knocked him off balance. "You mean, sexually?" he asked.

"Yeah." Her voice breathy, face playful, and wig easily recognizable.

"Yeah," he replied, "I get aroused at work."

"Really? How often?"

"I dunno. Occasionally."

"So, what do you do? You said you're not a cop."

"Nope," he interjected. "I'm an engineer."

"An engineer?" Luscious replied, with a lilt of faux delight.

"Yeah. Electrical. I design things to make life easier…for somebody, I guess."

"Okay. So, Mr. Engineer, how do you get off at work?"

She smiled. Bradley laughed. He sat back and took a drink "How do I get off at work? With my imagination," he said, turning again to look at her.

She nodded slowly with a mischievous smile. She sipped her fruity cocktail, a special concoction poured from the dancer-only bottle back at the bar to ensure a dancer didn't get drunk from all the free drinks.

"What about you? How do you get off at work?"

"Well, sometimes during a table dance or a couch dance, I'll straddle a guy's leg and ride it a lil' bit."

Even if it weren't true, he thought, it sure as hell sounded nice. The thought of her grinding away on his knee was certainly an image to behold. However, her response left him speechless. It would seem stilted, distasteful, and downright disrespectful to say something like, *You wanna ride my leg for a while*? Gentlemen weren't so crude. And to offer her a *horsey ride* would sound downright corny, if not altogether creepy.

"Okay," he grinned. "That beats my method."

"Mm. Does it?"

Just like that, Luscious was in control. She smiled. She smoked. She drank. And Bradley did too.

In the silence, Bradley sneaked another peek and marveled at the woman beside him. Her poise was on par with Abby's and just as appealing. As for her other attributes, Abby wasn't a dancer but that's not what drew them together to begin with. It was serendipity. They had met at a cocktail party hosted by Bradley's co-worker. Abby had shown up as the guest of a friend who was acquainted with the party's host. In the course the evening his eyes kept bumping into hers. He was the only black person at the party, and Abby would tell him a few weeks later that she was captivated by his confidence; at how perfectly at ease and in control he seemed amid the sea of white faces—candor he found refreshing and amusing. Bradley recalled how Abby stood apart from the crowd, too. Above-average height and thin, skinny to some, she had large eyes and a warm smile, her bobbed hair a shade of auburn. When they found themselves alone on the balcony (actually, Bradley watched Abby venture outside and pursued her), it was as though two strangers who had passed each other so many times before on the avenue were now waiting together at the bus stop. And finally, a name was attached to that familiar face he'd smiled at so many times before. A connection made, it was just the beginning.

Bradley hadn't come to The Cabaret looking to trade up, trade down, or even trade sideways. Or so he thought. If not for their unique and sometimes conflicting obligations—like Abby's Florida trip—he and Abby would likely be as one at home, reading quietly beside each other, discussing the news of the day, or cuddling and chuckling at another silly episode of Cheers; the make-believe TV tavern where all the white folks know each other's name. Instead, they had been pulled increasingly in opposite directions, leaving a gap that maybe could not be closed by a wedding after all leaving a space for Luscious to occupy.

"So," she said then, "you interested in a dance or what?"

"Yeah. I'm interested," he said, now more resigned than enthralled. "How much is a table dance?"

"Ten."

He dug out another ten-spot from his wallet and laid it on the table.

She waited for a song she liked, but eventually settled on some head-banger tune. She sat on his lap front-wards and back, even rubbed her tits in his face. And, as if to toss him a bone or merely assert her control, Luscious straddled his thigh a lil' bit. She smiled seductively the whole time as if to say, *This is how I'd do it if I were really digging you.* But for some reason Bradley could not really buy into the fantasy.

The dance seemed much less gratifying than watching her dance alone up there on the stage. And when she was through, it seemed there was little else left to say. He knew she wouldn't be going home with him. Even though he knew that going in, the reality of it disappointed him. Just like that, the ride was over. Any lingering satisfaction came not from sexual gratification, but from the freedom in knowing that at least he wouldn't have to worry about Abby picking up the scent of another woman. That also meant she wouldn't be present to relieve his tension once he got home.

Bradley tapped out another Marlboro Light, lit up, and rested back in the chair.

Meanwhile, Luscious sat down to put on her top and hot pants.

She took out another cigarette. As Bradley leaned forward and held a flame for her, she stared up into his eyes briefly, a Virginia Slim pressed to her purple lips. In that moment of her elongated inhalation, as the cigarette's embers grew more intense, Bradley saw tenderness in her face that he hadn't recognized previously.

Luscious sat back and exhaled a long trail of smoke as her eyes looked over his brown face from brow to chin to neck; nose to ear. "You know, you have nice ears. Nice lobes…Ever think about getting an earring?"

"No," he responded, meekly. "That's not me. Besides, I don't think I could pull it off."

"Really?" she asked earnestly. "You should think about it."

Charmed, Bradley sensed a reversal of fortunes for reasons that weren't clear. And in a burst of confidence, he asked: "So, what's your name? …I mean your real name?"

Luscious side-eyed him and smiled shrewdly, taken aback somewhat by the sudden forwardness. After a pause she returned absentmindedly to her previous thought, saying: "Yeah, you should think about it."

A polite way of saying, 'none of your damn business'? If he could have withdrawn the question, he would have. But it was too late.

Luscious then put her cigarette in the ashtray and reached into her purse to retrieve a pen. She scribbled seven digits on one of the unused napkins strewn on the table. She then reached for her drink and smoke.

Bradley claimed the napkin bearing a telephone number, minus a name.

"Humph. Okay," he said. "So, when is the best time to reach you?"

"I dunno. I'll let you decide, Mr. Engineer. But you know my work schedule. You know I work evenings."

He nodded affirmatively, thinking, *what's a girl like you*…before his thoughts trailed off.

Back at home, Bradley thought about if and when he might call on

Luscious. Tonight wasn't the night, though, and he placed her number on the dresser. He retreated to the bathroom and thought again about Luscious. He then summoned the memory of he and Abby together again. That did the trick. And having done that, he could finally sleep.

Thursday

Mama may have, Papa may have

13

The ceiling in conference rooms D and E was dark as a moonless, starless night. Red exit signs glowed like ranged lights above the two sets of double doors that sealed off the combined meeting space from the hotel outside. Traces of brightness filled the narrow gaps and crevices created where the wood-veneer doors came together to enclose the room.

As if they had seen it all before and knew what to expect, no one said a word, not even a murmur.

Meanwhile, a shadowy figure at the front of the room fiddled with the VCR.

"Okay," he said. "That should do it."

Moments later an explosion of light and sound lit up the room, like the sun announcing its rise.

"Whoa. I guess that's a wee bit loud," said the man. He moved quickly to lower the volume on the large screen television.

In keeping with the established pattern, the diversity instructor had popped in a video to dramatize a provisional exchange between several members of the minority troupe du jour talking among themselves before the players interacted with the white control group.

The day's discussion would focus on blacks in the morning followed by whites that afternoon.

Abby considered the day's topics the main event after a week's worth of under-card clashes.

It was certainly the area that most interested the *Daily News* editor when he settled on this idea of diversity training. Although various races and ethnicities were represented in the metropolitan area in varying degrees, there were no Asian-Americans or Native-Americans employed at the newspaper. Nor were there any Hispanics as far as one could tell, at least there were no Spanish surnames in the staff directory. No, the primary conflict and power struggles inside the *Daily News* newsroom and the community it served were between black folks and white folks. The burgeoning Hispanic population on city's eastside was not yet deemed disruptive enough.

Perhaps the editor knew something his subordinates did not. Perhaps, she allowed, he was something of a visionary.

The video opened with an attractive, milk-chocolate complexion woman talking to a black male associate as they prepared for a business meeting. She was clear in her aims and goals, while the man's personality was sketched in somewhat tentative strokes. On the other hand, he was also depicted as maybe more rational whereas the woman was a shown to be headstrong and a tad emotional. The man, in fetching a cup of coffee for them both, asked the woman how she took hers. The actor replied:

"I like my coffee the way I like my men—strong and black."

The comment elicited a scattering of chuckles.

The educational video later showed the two-person team negotiating a business deal across the table with several white businessmen. At one point, the black man appeared wobbly on certain terms he and his partner had previously discussed before ruling them out as unacceptable. She then stepped forward and with her eyes nudged him to be strong and black, her unspoken directives clear.

Here was a model of black womanhood—*sistahood*, Abby thought, whose representatives were seemingly immune to domestic belittlement at the hands of any of man. She found the piece implied perhaps non-African-American women, i.e. white women, were somehow less than, as was any black man who could not deal with such independent spirit. She sensed that steadfast attitude whenever a black woman took note of her union with Bradley, as if she was the would-be girlfriend the undeserving Abby had replaced; an affirmative action appointment, no doubt. The look said: *He's with you, honey, because he cannot handle a strong black sista like me.*

But what those women didn't know is Abby didn't iron Bradley's shirts either. She wanted to lash out: "He irons his own damn shirts or he wears them wrinkled or not at all!"

Over time, however, she had grown increasingly resistant to such female braggadocio she felt directed her way. Truth be told, in an odd way she sort of enjoyed the attention her interracial romance generated. It was similar to the minor thrill she got each time from seeing her byline in the paper. And it made people think, if only for a moment. It made people consider the possibilities.

Abby didn't invite any unnecessary scrutiny. When she dined the previous night with several female classmates, which included two black women, she didn't bother mentioning her fiancé's race, even though the subject of spouses came up and how men, they playfully noted, can be such worthless bastards. She would have had to force it into the conversation, making a gratuitous reference to race that violated her journalism training. News ethics, unlike private conversations involving people of the same race, dictate that a person's race not be noted in a story unless it's germane. She didn't want to take their otherwise pleasant, race-neutral dinner chat down that pockmarked road.

Abby felt wholly justified keeping that piece of herself private, particularly when the unmarried black woman in their party noted how a good man was hard to find.

She chose instead to absorb the atmosphere and imagined life in a more vibrant city, like Miami.

Abby accepted she probably would never work for the *New York Times*. Nevertheless, she felt increasingly restless where she was. Something had changed. The shred of optimism that existed when she and Bradley began their careers in the mid-1980s was gone. Perhaps it had been an illusion all along. She told Bradley she felt ready to try her hand somewhere else the last time they talked seriously about the direction of their careers.

Bradley wouldn't have any problem finding a new job, she thought. You just don't see too many black electrical engineers collecting unemployment. His prospects were probably much better than hers.

When her pal, Derrick, left the *Daily News* almost a year or so earlier, she was happy and jealous. She was happy a talented co-worker got a shot at a larger paper and disappointed she had been left behind. Not that he wasn't ready for such a move, but she was certain that being black helped his marketability. She was fine with that, for the most part. But in her most illiberal moods, she occasionally longed for an affiliate membership with the National Association of Black Journalists just to attend their job fairs. After all, hadn't she been asked more than once if she had some black in her? So why not reap the fringe benefits?

Bradley just asked her to be patient a little while longer. The timing wasn't right. Let him see this project through, he said, because it was good experience and good exposure. He also didn't want to appear as if he were bailing out of a situation whose outcome was uncertain. Moreover, the idea someone might try to cast him as some kind of racial opportunist was loathsome, he said.

Abby replied that he was being too short sighted.

Perhaps. But leaving also meant giving up seniority, Bradley countered, something the union lived and died for. Seniority had little meaning for him, however, until the day he overheard two millwrights talking near the coffee station about the possible changes in the next union contract. Rumor had it the new contract might tinker with a worker's seniority rights. The tradesmen were adamant in their opposition to anything that even remotely resembled seniority tampering.

"You start fucking with my seniority, and then I get mad," said one millwright to his nodding partner. "Because it's all I got. It's all I fucking got."

Bradley recalled: *Yeah, bruh, I feel ya,* as granules of non-dairy creamer transformed his dark, murky water into something even more opaque. He too had achieved a degree of seniority—racial seniority.

He was a known entity at Delcorp and within his department. Leaving meant starting over and having to go through the same old bullshit of having to prove himself a capable black man having secretaries eye him warily as he searched the stationary supply cabinet for manila folders. He longed to say: "I'm not gonna steal anything, dammit. I'm just looking for some goddamn folders and maybe a pen or two!"

Of course, he didn't. Still, those were blood-pressure-raising exercises he could do without for now.

So, Abby agreed to wait for now.

Inside conference rooms D and E, Walter Montgomery switched on the lights as the credits began to roll on the large television screen. Abby, along with many of her classmates, blinked and squinted as the electricity flowed to brighten the room.

Several others, however, catnapped a few moments longer. They opened their eyes once Scott English, the African-American instructor, began deconstructing this latest dramatization.

"Basically, this clip shows how African-American men and women tend to function more as equal partners when dealing with other people," he said. "This goes against the traditional model of our male-dominated society, where the male is portrayed as the undisputed head of a bi-gender unit. Think of shows like 'Ozzie and Harriet,' and 'Leave it to Beaver.' In contrast to those images, this matrilineal archetype that you've just witnessed has its origins in Africa. The legacy of slavery also plays a role in that; as we all know, men and women were often separated on the auction block. Black women had to be strong because black men weren't there to protect them in the classic American sense. Is everyone with me? Does this make sense?"

It makes perfect sense, Abby thought sardonically as her eyes came into focus: *This is what it means to be black.*

14

Bradley and Gary spent a portion of the morning watching raw spark plug insulators tumble out of the gentle grip of the robotic fingers that were supposed to transfer them smoothly from one indexing turntable to another.

For Bradley, he felt like a frustrated football coach watching his quarterback continually miss the open receiver on a simple pass route. Although the machine placed some parts successfully, there were far too many dropped insulators rolling around on the turntable base. Production efficiency and quality—victory, no less—demanded far better consistency.

The machine's intricate tooling was in place. The programmable logic controller was functioning and its program loaded. Before the day's slow-motion trial run, he and his electrician partner had spent most of the week testing the program's various logic conditions in an off-line mode to ensure the inputs and outputs performed on cue. So why isn't this damn thing working, he wondered.

The automated equipment was supposed to complete the detailed sequence of operations with the same precision of the prototype machine and the first machine installed on line one. However, taking a piece of equipment from the test room to the shop floor was rarely accomplished with flawless execution. Implementation could be stalled by a variety of real-world conditions. Simply moving the heavy machinery into place could knock a key limit switch out of whack or damage an electronic sensor.

Having failed to adequately diagnose what might be causing the machine's frequent miscues, Bradley and Gary took a short field trip over to line one to once again observe its operation and glean a few ideas. And, if nothing else, simply seeing another machine in operation would remind the duo of the possibilities.

Line one was only partially operable, as the plant's construction crew was still finishing up work on the downstream systems on the automated assembly line. But the main portion where the spark plug insulators were assembled had been completed, and sample parts were already being run.

Bradley watched the complete operation, beginning at the point where the raw insulators started their journey. Propelled by the force of controlled vibration, the pale white, tubular insulators rattled up and out of the spiral feeder bowl single file like a snake uncoiling itself. The insulators continued upwards to a metal track where they then fell vertical and tottered down the track towards a mechanical dropper. The shaking tubular parts lined up and rattled like anxious boys awaiting physicals. Meanwhile, the large turntable fitted with narrow spindles along its edges indexed forward one spindle at a time. One by one, the mechanical dropper lowered the insulators onto the spindles during the fraction of a second when the indexing turntable paused.

Pssst. Pssst. Pssst. Pssst.

Each turn of the table corresponded to the air blast—*Pssst, Pssst, Pssst*—that washed the insulators clean of any loose particles that hadn't fallen off when the insulators were lowered onto the spindles. The insulators were rubbed by an ink stamp that stenciled the letters DVS on their bodies. As each insulator-capped spindle proceeded methodically to the next stage, they began spinning in preparation for station three.

Shhht. Shhht. Shhht. Shhht.

A spray gun coated the spinning insulators with a dusty-blue layer of glazing that would be baked into a clear, lustrous finish once the plug bodies completed their ride through the 1500-degree furnace at the end of the assembly line. As the machine continued indexing, the parts passed a small camera, which, in the blink of an eye, checked the stenciling and glazing operations.

Bradley was especially proud of the machine-vision station. It was his little contribution to the operation. Without it, the machine had no way of knowing whether a part to be transferred off the first turntable was defective or lacking preparation. The parts weren't being inspected until much later in the process when mistakes became more costly to fix. But he said why not inspect the parts sooner, like right after they pass through the glazing stage? He borrowed the idea from an operator working on one of the obsolete lines, soon to be replaced by the new automated equipment. He noticed how she made a quick visual inspection, looking for cosmetic imperfections, before manually loading the insulators into a tray. Any part that didn't meet her standards got tossed into a scrap bin. That's what the automated machine lacked, he thought. It didn't have eyes, at least not where it should.

The vision system took care of that. And the electronic eyes went one better. The camera not only inspected the parts; it provided more exacting and consistent scrutiny. Thus, the human variable was further contained. He also wrote a subroutine for the machine's PLC program, which essentially told the robotic hand how to behave when it plucked a defective part; dump it. But at that moment, there were no rejects as the machine continued cycling.

Click-clank. Click-clank. Click-clank. Click-clank.

The robotic hand lifted the stenciled-and-glazed insulators individually from their spindles on turntable one and gracefully translocated the parts to a series of sockets on turntable number two to begin the second stage of the assembly process. First, metal pins were dropped down the center of the hollow bodies, leaving a tiny portion exposed at end to form the electrode. The electrode is where the ignition spark would occur once the finished plug is screwed into an engine block.

Meanwhile, a cavity was created in the interior of the insulator. The cavity was first filled with a calibrated dash of fine, gray semi-metallic powder and the volume was then tamped as if packing a cannon. The powder-and-tamp routine was repeated at a subsequent station. Finally, the terminal stud—the point to which the engine's distributor wire is attached—was stuffed into the end.

The unfinished spark plugs resembled tiny soldiers carrying rifles with fixed bayonets on their shoulders. These little soldiers were then off-loaded from the second turntable into a single-file line on a vibrating track. As a line of spark plugs formed on the track, a five-finger mechanical paw grabbed a fist full of five and placed them into a waiting metal tray. The tray indexed forward slightly as each row was filled with five plugs.

Once all six rows were loaded, the boatload of thirty tiny soldiers was shoved toward the end of the conveyor like a D-Day landing craft motoring onward toward the beaches of Normandy. There at the end, a two-handed robotic busboy transferred the tray to another conveyor to begin its long, slow ride through hell—a glowing, 1,500-degree kiln that baked the stenciled-and-glazed insulators into glossy ceramic spark plugs.

Bradley observed the entire sequence of operations and marveled at the technological know-how that made it all possible. The tooling. The electronics. The pneumatics. The hydraulics. They all blended together in harmony, bringing together disparate materials to create something altogether different and new.

The critics could say all they wanted about the American automobile industry, but *we've got some pretty smart people, too,* Bradley thought.

"Hey, you know what?" Gary said. "I'd bet you anything the cam switch that's firing the pick-and-place is off a bit. See, look at the machine's position as the pick-and-place gets ready to grab the insulator. See where it is?"

Click-clank. Click-clank.

"I think ours is out of position a taste," Gary said.

Bradley zeroed in on the pick-and-place. It was a simple operation, but the sequence of steps became trickier when a timing mechanism came into play. A cam switch energized the coil that fired the solenoid. The solenoid activated the pneumatic cylinder, which drove the robot's mechanical functions to rise, lower, grip, and release.

"Mm-hmm. Yeah. I bet you're right," said Bradley. "I don't know why we didn't think of that before."

Click-clank. Click-clank.

"Well, there are so many other things to consider on these high-tech puppies that you sometimes overlook the easy stuff."

The twosome studied the pick-and-place mechanism a few moments longer only to confirm their conclusions and make sure they hadn't overlooked anything else.

"Whelp, that'll give us a good place to start this afternoon," said Gary. "It's dinner time. I'll see you in forty-five minutes or so."

He turned and walked away.

Gary moseyed across the street to his favorite lunchtime watering hole. Bradley, meanwhile, trotted off in a different direction to a visit a nearby Mexican restaurant, opened recently.

After three cold, gray days, the sun had finally managed to find an opening in which to peek through. It wasn't expected to hang around for long, however. The newspaper warned of a strong possibility for snow flurries on Friday and Saturday.

Bradley dined alone at the counter on the beef burrito lunch special while an elevated television blathered on and on about nothing of consequence. The local news station then teased viewers with tidbits of a story slated for the noon telecast.

> *"We'll have a live report from the county courthouse where the trial of three men accused of dangling a scarecrow from a bridge overpass onto the freeway is nearing a conclusion. We'll have that story, plus your weekend forecast. So stay with us."*

The ever-cheerful noon TV anchor spoke as if she were hosting a viewing party instead of a news broadcast.

Gary apparently saw the same news brief, or something similar, while having a beer and burger with his buddies because it was the first item on his agenda once he and Bradley returned to job site.

"Have you kept up at all with that trial?"

"A little bit. Why?"

"I think the prosecutor is being a little heavy-handed with those boys."

Bradley exhaled a cloud of cigarette smoke. "How so?"

"I think it was a prank that just got out of hand. Now, it's unfortunate that woman had to lose her life, but I don't believe those boys meant to cause any harm. If they want to punish them, I think they ought to give 'em probation or community service, if they're convicted. I say, save the prisons for the drug dealers and real criminals."

"Mmm. I guess that's one way of looking at it."

"What do you think?"

"Well, I don't know. It probably was a prank, but then someone died. So that changes things, you know?"

"Yeah, but I don't think there should be the big trial that's going on and all this talk about those boys doing jail time."

"Well, would it have been okay if one of those guys were driving drunk and killed someone?"

"Those boys probably were drinking that night when they pulled that stunt." Gary laughed.

"That's not what I asked."

"Oh, I know. You're talking about drunk driving." Gary changed his tack. "Well, let me ask you something. What if there had been an actual person out there that night walking on the freeway and the driver ran off the road as she swerved to miss him. Should that guy be prosecuted and thrown in jail?"

"I don't see that as the same thing. No," as he thought about it further, "that's not the same thing at all. Those guys may not have been trying to hurt someone, but they were certainly trying to scare someone, I think. And they're grown men. They should have known better than to do something stupid like hanging a scarecrow onto the highway."

"Okay then. Let's say he was stumbling around drunk on the highway."

"That's still not the same thing. If you're standing on the road like some kind of drunken idiot, the person you're likely to hurt is yourself."

"Not unless someone runs off the road while trying to avoid killing you. And that takes us back to the scarecrow incident."

"Nah," said Bradley, shaking his in disagreement before changing his tack. "Okay. Look, if you want to prosecute the drunken fool who stumbles down onto a highway and scares someone into running off the road, causing their death or serious injury, fine. Prosecute him, too."

Bradley flicked ash from his cigarette before taking a puff. After a quick exhale, he said: "I don't know if those guys will be found guilty or not. I'm not a lawyer. But I think the charges were probably warranted. From what I've read, I don't think the woman would have run off the road if she didn't think there was someone standing in the middle of the road."

"Well, I think that prosecutor is just trying to make a name for himself. Same thing with that incident that happened up there on the northside this week. That fella shouldn't be charged with anything. He was just protecting himself and his family. I applaud that fella for making a stand. That's the trouble with this city. More people aren't willing to take a stand and say, 'Dammit, enough is enough.'

Bradley glared. Gary continued.

"Yeah, and I think we ought to be allowed to carry guns. I think it would cut down on a lot of this bullshit you see going on nowadays. If a guy knows you're armed, I guarantee he'll think twice about trying to rob you."

"Well, he *was* armed and *still* got robbed."

"Yeah, well, he never should have let his guard down. He should have kept his distance. And he should have kept his jacket open so if he needed to grab his gun, he could get to it quickly."

"Is that right?"

"But, mainly, he should have kept his distance. You know?"

Bradley studied the man's face for clues but said nothing. He dropped a spent cigarette on the factory floor, grinding out the embers beneath his foot. He then looked up and exhaled a cloud of smoke.

"Shall we get back to work?"

Bradley was seated at his desk finishing up some notations on the electrical schematic when his telephone went off like an alarm bell.

"Bradley Cunningham," he said.

"*Bradley?*"

"What?"

"Have you heard?" Abby said. Her two-toned voice expressed shock and excitement.

"Heard what?" the non-journalist replied. "What's the matter?"

"…He announced this afternoon that he's HIV-positive. He's retiring."

"*What?* Magic!? Are you kidding me? Does he have AIDS?"

"No. As I understand it, it's the AIDS virus. We found out during our break this afternoon. That's all everyone wanted to talk about. So I started taking notes and called the paper and fed them some quotes for a round-up story they're doing. I think I'll blow off the rest of the afternoon session. We were just talking about white people in America, so I figured I didn't need to hear about that, anyway…I just cannot believe that he's has the AIDS virus."

Bradley said nothing. The factory noise seemed to vanish and everything else suddenly seemed small and insignificant. His thoughts on premature death.

"Wow. I mean, you just don't think things like that can happen to people like him."

"Oh, I know. I know. I remember when Rock Hudson came out and announced he had AIDS? But that was different. I guess because he was of another generation and not someone that we really paid much attention to. But with him, he seems like such a nice guy and such a role model."

In other words, they each thought; this is our generation. This is real.

"Yeah," said a dazed Bradley.

"Then, it turns out that Rock Hudson was gay. But with him…" her voice trailed off. "He said he contacted it from a woman."

"Humph."

The conversation ceased as the factory sounds re-emerged to fill the void. They were both thinking the same thing, but neither one wanted to say it. Their reticence was out of respect for a person that neither really knew, except through television. And talking about his condition too much, specifically how he contacted the virus, threatened to dredge up topics couples prefer not to discuss.

In that moment of silence, Bradley thought about every woman, domestic or foreign, he had ever been with. He even recalled the time he and Abby stopped using condoms.

She finally broke the silence; her tone almost apologetic. "You think he's bisexual or something?"

"Uh…I don't know. I guess I never thought about it before… Well, wait a minute, I dunno," he decided, finally. "Why? Do you?"

"Well, he said he got it from a woman. But I guess it really doesn't matter at this point, huh?"

But it did matter. Secretly, they both hoped he was at least bisexual. That way, as lifelong heterosexuals, it would be one less thing to worry about. Life would be easier, less complicated. The hierarchy would set them apart; set them free of worry.

"Yeah, well, wow. I'm just shocked."

"Me too."

"Did I ever tell you about the time I met him?"

"Huh? No. When?"

Bradley could once again hear that two-toned voice of a journalist.

"I guess it was one of those things that just happened. It was no big deal really. Anyway, it was some years ago at a summer engineering program I attended at State. Me and some other people were walking back from lunch when someone yelled he was outside. We didn't believe it until we went to the door and saw this huge guy towering over everyone else. He was signing autographs and everything," said Bradley, as he recalled how the giant looked like a dog owner preparing to feed a bunch of hungry puppies.

"Did you get his autograph?"

"Nah. Everyone else was out there trying to get it and he said had to get going. I didn't press it. But he shook my hand before he hopped back into his Benz and left. That was good enough for me. You know, it was one of the moments where you say to yourself, 'Wow, he really seems like a nice guy.' Man, I hope he's going to be all right."

"Oh, I know," said Abby. "Well, I'm going to get going."

"Yeah, and I need to finish up some stuff here before I leave."

"Okay, well, I'll talk to you later. I love you, Brad."

"Love you too, hon."

Bradley got off the phone and thought, damn. He felt a need to share the news with someone and saw Gary locking up his toolbox and preparing to hit the showers. Gary's face lost all colour when he heard the news.

"Are you *shittin'* me?" said Gary, as if questioning the Fates.

15

Thursday night was supposed to be a night to chill and maybe catch up on some reading before Abby's return the following day. Bradley figured a rest was in order since he had been playing bachelor all week. He even dined at home on a burger and fries he made himself.

But James convinced his "big bruh" to spend a night on the town with him, arguing they hadn't seen each other in weeks nor "hung together in like forever."

When Bradley tried to put him off until the weekend, James pushed back.

"See, man, Polly's gonna be back in town, your dick's gonna be all hard and you won't have no time for this brotha. And it'll be another two weeks before we can even think about brewing it up together. In fact, I had to find out from Pops that your overseer was even out of town—"

"Overseer? What? Man, later for you, J."

"What's up with that, man? You can't call a brotha?"

"You're right, man. My fault. I got your message today, by the way."

"Aw, man, don't apologize. Let's hang. Old man!"

Once Bradley acquiesced, a triumphant James said: "Bet. I'll scoop you in a half. I'm out your way, anyway, checkin' out a honey."

James arrived ten minutes earlier than expected, which was quite surprising since one typically had to add at least a half hour to James' agreed upon time of arrival.

"B-Nice! Whassup, boy-ee!" James said when his brother opened the front door.

James stepped inside and the brothers immediately locked

hands in a soul brother's grip while using their free arms to pull each other into an embrace.

He was a more muscular version of his older sibling. In high school, James roamed the gridiron as a rover back—a sort of hybrid linebacker-defensive back. They called it the "monster back". Asked once at the barbershop how many interceptions he had snatched as a player, James replied modestly, "A couple." He then quickly added, "My specialty was knockouts." The Marines added more bulk to his frame.

After separating and shaking off the cold, he wasted no time poking at his older brother's musical tastes. "Man, what is that shit you're listening to?"

"Jimi?" said Bradley, referring to the sound of Jimi Hendrix's *Foxy Lady* playing in the background. "Don't you know there ain't one white boy alive who wouldn't suck Jimi's dick?" he said with the typical awkwardness his voice carried whenever he tried to talk raunchy.

"Oh, I forgot. That's why you like that shit. Yeah, all right, Clarence Thomas." James laughed as he trotted out of the reach of his brother's quick jab.

Forced to rely on words and not his fists, Bradley took aim at his brother's all-black attire—mock turtleneck, trousers, leather jacket, and pager. His left lobe was pierced with a shimmering diamond-studded earring and his short Afro was faded out on the sides until the hair simply vanished.

"Forget you, J, you fake Black Panther with your cubic zirconium earring. What? You couldn't afford the matching beret and pump shotgun, punk?"

"Naw, man, just fuckin' with you. You know you and Jimi are my boys. Eh, man," said James, shifting gears and turning serious, "is that jacked or what about our boy? Oh, man. Dude just got married and everything. He's giving up ball."

James opened the beer he found in the refrigerator and took a swig. He then shook his head.

"I know. When Abby called to tell me, I was speechless."

"Man, it was *THE* topic of conversation this afternoon at the barbershop. Brothas were in absolute *dis-be-lief*. Even C.T. was in chill mode. One dude, though, tried to say he got infected because he's been taking it in the tailpipe. He was talking all loud and shit. And you know Daddy-O wasn't hearing that noise. Pops was like: 'Mister, please kindly. Calm. The fuck. Down.'"

Bradley chuckled and shook his head. "How was dad otherwise?"

"Like everyone else. Shocked. Surprised. Sad. Hoping for the best and that the brotha keeps on livin'. You know?" James gulped some beer. "Me too."

The brothers fell silent while Jimi filled the void.

...I gonna take you home, uh-huh.
I won't do you no harm, no...

"By the way, did you pay dad back? He said you owed him so money."

"Man, yeah. I paid him. Man, Pops is trippin'; always tryin' to sweat a brotha."

"Right."

"Yeah, so anyway, Pops told me Polly is in Florida all week. She's at a conference or something?"

"Yeah. Diversity training."

"Diversity training? What the- What's that all about?"

"I guess it's supposed to show how people of different races can all get along and communicate better at work."

"Get the fuck outta here. That's diversity training?" James grinned. "So what's that like a twelve-step program or something?"

"Yeah, I guess," Bradley chuckled. He turned up his beer bottle.

"'Hi, my name is Mr. Charlie and I'm a racist,'" James blurted, imagining it as a Racists Anonymous meeting. "'Hi, Mr. Charlie!'" he added, imitating Mr. Charlie's fellow racists in class.

Bradley nearly spat beer before folding over with restrained laughter. His mouth dripped at the corners. After wiping his mouth with the back of his hand, he said: "I told Abby she could have tested out of the course."

"No shit. Square biz, though. What is she doing, giving a presentation or something?"

The brothers shared another hearty laugh and tapped their

clenched fists together as if pounding five.

"Yeah, I heard that," said James, still amused and in a zone of his own. "Polly—I mean, Abby—" He grinned.

"Thank you."

"Abby was like: 'Yeah. I'll take a free trip to Florida for diversity's sake, dammit, for the cause.' I'll tell you what. She picked a good week to be there 'cause it's been colder than a *motherfucker* this week."

16

James, the self-styled truth-teller about America, the beautiful, took it upon himself to welcome Abby into the family with a bit of brotherly love. He did so by renaming her, in confidence with Bradley, Polly—short for "Sweet Polly Purebred."

Sweet Polly Purebred, the ever-damsel-in-distress, was the girlfriend of the cartoon character Underdog, whose superhero body resembled a sack of flour propped up on a pair of stubby stilts. Recalling his funny looking physique, James jokingly asked his brother once if he thought Underdog ever hit that ass.

That Abby and Polly were both reporters was purely coincidental. James in fact had forgotten, until being reminded sometime later, that Polly Purebred was a newspaper reporter. No, he called Abby "Polly" because, he said, Polly Purebred exemplified the so-called purity of white womanhood that must be protected.

Abby was offended, of course, when she discovered her codename. She resented the idea that someone would dare characterize her that way and vented her anger at Bradley. Although James never used the name in her presence, she took it as evidence of his dislike or disrespect of her. Bradley explained his brother meant it affectionately. Abby wasn't buying it, though.

"Really, that's the way brothers do it." He added the name, in James' mind, merely described the way society likes to portray white women—especially those who might date a black man. That's all. Just call him "Riff Raff," Bradley advised.

As far as white people in general, James admitted he wasn't particularly crazy about the abstraction. His exact words to Bradley were

"I do not like those motherfuckers. I do not trust them." Bradley, however, could appreciate his kid brother's hyperbolism.

James shocked the family by joining the Marines right out of high school. He said he was tired of school but was unsure of what he wanted to do. Ellis, meanwhile, told his youngest son that drifting around town waiting for trouble to find him wasn't an option. He had to do something. So, James one day up and joined the military.

He was inducted in August 1983. By late October of that year elements of the 82nd Airborne dropped into Grenada, along with some U.S. Army Rangers and Special Forces, to make that Caribbean island "a safe place again for tourists and third-rate medical school students," according to James. His jocularity, however, disappeared whenever someone inquired about the suicide bombing of the U.S. Marine barracks in Lebanon that same year. He had few words say about it, beyond: "That was really fucked up. We never should have been hung out there like that." And that would be it.

James was all but certain that President Reagan was out to get him personally, seeking to use him as some kind of pawn to re-establish America's flaccid manhood. So, he did his three years then "got the fuck out of Dodge because Ronny baby was too damn trigger-happy for this brotha. The commercials said the military was a great place to start. They didn't say jack about fightin' and killin' and dyin'," he said. Recounting his military service, he referred to it as having paid his debt to society "because I love the way that fucks with white folks' heads."

In all seriousness, the experience gave him valuable time to think and something in which to lose himself until he was ready to resurface. After being discharged in the mid-1980s, James returned home and enrolled in community college to study graphic design and eventually found a job with an outdoor advertising agency, work he thoroughly enjoyed.

Sometime later he would decide the money he'd been burning on dime bags to medicate his periodic bouts with misery could be better spent elsewhere. A portion of the money, in due time, would be redirected to cover the co-pay for occasional visits to a psychologist.

When it became apparent that Bradley intended to marry that white babe, "Polly," James asked his brother if he were trying to live out King's dream.

Bradley remembered their conversation like it was yesterday. Its memory hung with him like the stifling humidity on a dull Michigan summer day.

They had met for drinks, sitting for what seemed like hours on the terrace of the hotel bar under a bright, broiling sun. The two men downed a time-consuming-succession of Long Island Iced Teas while laughing, joking, and telling stories and half-truths about all the pussy they'd known. Like the time they watched a rented porno tape with those two women they had met at the bar one night.

"Man, I'm telling you: those hoes were into that flick," James recalled. "Am I right?"

They laughed in agreement and moved on, further back in time, to that day they were busted raiding the Henry's pear tree. Mr. and Mrs. Henry were supposed to be gone.

"We were trying to hug the tree to blend in with the leaves, like Mr. Henry couldn't see us up there when he came outside. He was like: Y'all caught. Y'all caught. I see you boys up there."

Yes, James said. He remembered. "Mr. Henry said, 'I'ma tell you boys' daddy on you two.' And I was like: Well, fuck me!"

The brothers were moved to tears as they recalled a hilarious skit from Richard Pryor's ill-fated television show. Pryor, playing the nation's first black president, is made comically and painfully aware that a post-racial America was pure fantasy. And, of course, they remembered their mother with the clinking of the glasses of their Long Island Iced Teas in her honour.

Then things got real all over again, as James wondered aloud if Bradley had really considered everything and false promises of racial harmony. The eldest brother tried to assure James that, indeed, he had.

"Yeah, well, you know, you've always been on the snow."

"Aw, man, like you've never hooked up with a white babe."

"Overseas," James said, to make a point about things being wholly different outside the good ol' U-S-of-A. "Yeah, I hit the slopes once or twice. Spent a lil' time in the Alps, ya' know? It's all part of my equal opportunity package. See, federal law states that in order to be a true player, you must also be an equal opportunity lover. Dick don't discriminate in the dark. Besides, Rollo likes his freedom." He then leaned toward Bradley and added: "But dig. Just between you and me

I may hit the ass, but no white babe will ever occupy my executive suite. Know what I'm sayin'?" He smiled and winked.

Kidding aside, James circled back and wanted to know if Bradley knew what he had gotten himself into.

Again, the answer was yes. But he added such questions annoyed him, although his frustration wasn't directed at James.

"After a while, you just start to think why does it always have to be, 'Yo, I'm a black man.'? Why can't it just be, 'Hey, I'm a man. I'm just a regular fella. My name is Bradley Cunningham'?"

"Why? I'll tell you why. Because that's the way the white folks see it—see you, see me."

Bradley said nothing while James gulped his drink.

James then continued: "You know, I read something recently about this woman who's battling alcoholism. She said the hardest thing about the recovery process was holding onto her own identity. She said, 'I don't want to be known as a recovering alcoholic for the rest of my life.' I thought it was an interesting comment. Basically, what she was saying is that regardless of what else she might be going through or what else she may be about as a person, she was concerned that, in the eyes of everyone else, her alcoholism would override all things about her. And I thought to myself, *Wow. Now she has some idea of what it's like to be black or African-American.*"

The older brother swallowed and listened.

"Except, there's a key difference: Few people probably would have known about her drinking problem if she hadn't revealed it in the article. You wouldn't necessarily know it if she walked into a room. See, what I'm saying is that we don't have that option of concealing who we are, bruh, unless you're light, bright, and almost white—and with good hair. That excludes you and that excludes me. And white folks take advantage of that shit. They do and you know it's true. It's not like religion or if you're a gay dude. Most times, you can hide that shit. Take the Jews. A lot of times I can't tell a Jew from your average Joe Whiteman. Shit, man, they're just white people to me; just another group of white people. Maybe back in the day it really mattered. But now? *Psssh.* I don't think so."

"That's not what the Klan says," said Bradley.

"Man, *fuck* the Klan," he snapped. "Anyway, the same thing

goes for your gay boys, unless they're just out cold with their shit. You don't really know who's with it or not. See what I'm saying?"

Bradley said nothing but drank some more.

"I love it when you hear them motherfuckers say, 'I don't care if you're black, white, green, purple, or have polka-dots,' James continued, mimicking a self-righteous white man. "Yeah right. *Bullshit.* I'd like to be around those same motherfuckers the first time they lay eyes on someone with green, purple, or polka-dotted skin. And don't let 'em be black with polka dots, dammit. Then they're really fucked."

Bradley laughed. James extended his fist and, as if banging a gavel, tapped it on Bradley's clenched fist.

"But hold on, J. Back up. There's a problem with your alcohol-addiction analogy. First of all, blackness isn't some kind of disease or an addiction."

"See, now, I didn't say that."

"Secondly, who's to say that's all anyone else would really see in her? Her drinking problem, that is. I don't accept that. Now, that's not to say she wouldn't run across an asshole or two who would make an issue of it. You deal with them or not. But you move on, just the same. That's all I'm saying. Hold on, I'm not through," said Bradley, when his brother's body language indicated he had something to say. "The way I see it, black pride is largely a, I dunno, private matter."

"Bullll-*shit!*"

"No, really."

"Man, that's some complete, unadulterated *bullshit.*" James grimaced. "Man, to white folks we are nothing but motherfucking public property to be used how they see fit...Ooh, man. What the fuck, B?" James looked askance at Bradley.

"No really. I mean, yeah, I'm proud to be black and all. You know that. But that's not all there is to me. And I don't feel a need to shove it in people's faces either. You know why?"

"Why?"

"Because I don't want them shoving their shit in my face. I don't. You know how you have these jokers talking about their European ancestry and the fucking old country. My feeling is: 'Sooo what? Big deal? You're here now; right here. If the old country was so goddamn great, then take your asses back over there and stay. Besides, a brotha could use your job.' But you know me. I don't make a big deal about it. I smile. I'll humor them and let them think that I really give a shit about what they're talking about. I don't make a big-to-do when they start yapping about how their granddaddies or great-granddaddies had to deal with anti-immigrant BS when they got off the boat, and how they had to Americanize their names and drop their accents to get over."

"See. You're too nice. I let 'em know."

"Yeah, maybe so. That's all right, though. That's all right. Just the same, I don't have to sit around and light candles on Martin Luther King's birthday or Abraham Lincoln's birthday."

"So what're you sayin', dog? James chuckled. "You don't think the good reverend doctor deserves a national holiday?"

"No, that's not what I'm saying. But honestly, I could take it or leave it. Besides, before long we'll be celebrating it with an 'I Have A Dream' super sale at Highland Appliance. And you'll still have some dumbass sales clerk trying to carefully analyze your signature if you try to pay for your purchase with anything other than cash," Bradley said. "I was at a store one time and this fool did that—examined the two signatures side by side. As soon as he gave me his approval and handed back the credit card, I said 'Ha. I just fooled another one.'"

James laughed and nodded as he swallowed.

"I was like, even if I had stolen the card, this fool doesn't know how long I might have been practicing the signature to get it passable. If you're gonna label me a criminal, at least give me more credit than that. I'm not that damn stupid, you know? But the point is, he's not qualified to judge the authenticity of my signature or me."

Bradley turned up his glass.

James nodded. "Yeah, I always like it when you get ready to pay for something and these motherfuckers automatically assume you're paying by cash. 'Will that be cash?' And you just heard the clerk ask the white ho in line in front of you if she'll be paying by cash, check or, or putting it on her Hudson's charge. I think to myself, fuck you. Fuck you people," he said, accenting the statement with a sharp middle-finger salute.

"Yeah, for real. Treat me with respect. That's all I'm saying. But don't try to BS me."

"Word," said James, who wet his throat again. His sip was relatively long and he stared at Bradley the whole time. He lowered the drink and then said, "Bradley Cunningham—the secret double agent." Bradley raised his drink in a tipsy toast to himself.

"Bradley Cunningham: *The Motown Man*." James laughed. The alcohol prevented him from leaving well enough alone.

"Motown Man?" Bradley stopped. "What's up with that?"

"Nothing, only that you're an agreeable and likeable kind of brotha. So you're like Motown music for all these white folks and before these Republican motherfuckers started talking all that shit about taking back America from, from…from something—from us," he decided.

"So, what? You trying to crack now? Or what?"

"No, not at all. Just an observation," said James, adjusting his posture. "I've been thinking about this for a little bit. And after hearing you talk just now, the pieces just fell together. Dig: We black folks tend to be defined by three styles of music we created. White folks need their stereotypes to deal with us because they don't have anything else to go on and finding out the real deal would be too fucking hard."

"Okay," said Bradley, his usual self returned.

"So, anyway, 'blackness' to whites is best defined by our music. Black gospel music, the Negro spiritual, equals the deep down, serious, hardworking, honest-to-goodness, you-can-beat-me-down-'cause-I'll-get-my-reward-in-Heaven black. The noble beast. America's burden. America's shame."

Bradley was silent.

"Next up: The Motown sound. It's for those lighter moments. It's the music of promise. See, it's what they played during the civil rights movement at the after-march parties—there's always an after party somewhere. White folks love to throw on some Motown music, don't they? Man, I was at this white wedding with a honey a while back. The DJ put on some old Motown jam and these white folks got up and were like '*Hallelujah*!'"

Bradley chuckled reflectively.

"At least that's what they play when there's an integrated crowd in the house, meaning there are two or three of us in a room filled with dozens of them motherfuckers. I don't know what they play when we're not around. Anyway, put on some Motown music and watch the white hoes gather for their pajama party on the dance floor while the white guys stand on the sidelines with a beer in one hand and the other one stuffed in their pants' pocket, searching for their nuts. Man, that shit trips me out the way white babes dance together like that. It's kind of freaky too, you know? 'Specially when they're all fine. I'm like, 'Yo, why don't we all roll back to the crib. We can put on some Motown sounds and twist and shout all…night…*long*." He laughed.

"Yeah, all right funny boy, Bradley chuckled. "And number three?"

"Why rap, of course. The harder, the deffer, the better. Rap defines today's black America, and provides the authentic underclass, inner-city—yeah, I like that word—'inner-city'. It's the inner-city experience for the cool white kids. Now white boys, just because they've heard a rap jam, think it's cool to call you 'chief' or 'ma' man' or 'homey.' 'What's up, chief?' 'Here you go ma' man.' And I say, 'Naw, here you go ma' man'," said James, grabbing his crotch.

The gesture of dominance and defiance—grabbing one's crotch—always seemed oddly homosexual, Bradley thought, even though it was meant to communicate the target was actually his bitch.

"So, let me get this straight," said Bradley after a pause. "You have the gospel black, the Motown black, and the rap black."

"Bingo. Gospel black equals good, hardworking, and selfless, and you're threatening only to the extent that you might want to vote or move in next door. The Motown black is decent, easy-going, and non-threatening, unless of course you're trying to get your groove on with Sweet Polly Purebred. The rapper is unemployed, at least not legitimately. He's remote, indifferent, and packin', if you're a brotha, or carrying a baby if you're a sista. Those are the choices, bruh. That's why you're a Motown man. I guess your only drawback is that you're not only dancing with Polly, you're bonin' her too."

"Mm-humph. So who are you, the rapper?"

"Right you are, ma' brotha', or should I say, *ma' man*. But that's okay 'cause these white folks don't know what time it is, man," said James, extending the gavel; Bradley obliged him.

James then paused to swallow more watered-down alcohol.

"Ahhh. Nope, they don't know what time it is…They don't

know the real me."

The brothers paused while James gulped down more Long Island Tea. Bradley eyed his brother and thought how James had never forgotten nor forgiven that carload of white guys for spraying him in the face with Mace when he was a boy. Once it seemed as if every white guy he encountered were riding in that car that summer afternoon so many years ago. They had claimed to be looking for a street address, but they were only really looking for a black boy to humiliate. They found James, who was pedaling his bicycle across that bowling alley's parking lot. "Take that you little nigger," they laughed, before speeding off.

James came home with tears leaking from his scrunched eyes, crying—"why they have to do that to me?"—and talking about how he was going "to beat somebody's butt," and feeling utterly helpless.

James joked it was his Jewish blood that wouldn't allow him to forget the experience, "'cause Jews don't forget shit, either."

In the silence that followed, Bradley felt an urge to reassure his kid brother. He threw his hand up in gesture of surrender and flashed a bashful, sincere smile.

"What can I say, man? I'm in love."

Bradley then told James he wouldn't be losing a brother but gaining a sister.

"In-law only," James retorted. "Sister-*in-law*. But she's not a *sista!*"

They laughed and pounded fists before toasting the occasion.

"Look here, B. Congratulations, man. Straight up."

James punctuated his sincerity by extending the fist gavel. Abby was getting a down brother, he said, and made it clear he had great affection for her, too.

"Yeah, Polly's my girl. So, if you all are happy, I'm happy. And, of course, you know I'm always gonna have your back...*Motown Man.*"

Bradley acknowledged him with a sly chin-up head nod.

"Yeah," James added, "just think of me as your Funk Brothers, all in one."

17

Inside the Cunningham abode in Grand Heights, the brothers worked on finishing their brews before hitting the bar scene. Bradley slipped away momentarily to finish prepping for their night on the town while James moved into the living room and switched the television on and the stereo off.

An episode of Cheers lit up the room, drawing James into the characters' weekly nonsense. He stood lording over the set even as Bradley re-emerged from the bedroom area.

"You ready?"

"Yeah," James mumbled, rather absentmindedly. His eyes transfixed on the screen below, he aimed the remote control at the set with an outstretched arm, pausing briefly like an executioner hearing a final plea before pulling the trigger. "You know, it's funny. You expect white folks to be like those you see on these witty TV shows and in the movies—beautiful, sophisticated, down for the cause. You know?"

He spoke to no one in particular and pressed the off switch. The room darkened; silence reigned.

"Ready?"

"Yeah. Let's do this, B," said James, and to the door they headed.

On his way out, James blew a kiss at a portrait of a woman displayed on the fireplace mantel—their mother's photograph taken a year or so before her death.

Outside, James switched on the ignition to his Toyota Celica convertible and a radio announcer shouted with over-the-top enthusiasm:

Coming to Douglass Theatre, for a limited engagement, the hit gospel musical 'Negro, please!'

A snippet of the play immediately followed.

"You say you gonna ask 'da Lord to help you pick 'da right lottery numbers? Negro, please! God don't work 'dat way!"

Uproarious laughter bellowed from the speakers.

Don't miss 'Negro, please.' Tickets available…

James chuckled. "So, B, you going to check that out? You and Polly?"

Bradley laughed.

"You're like: 'Yeah right,'" said James, answering his own question. "Abby would be like, 'You wanna go where? *Negro, please!*'"

James began rummaging through a case of cassette tapes. He slid a tape into the mouth of the player and threw the car into reverse. "Need some theme music for this hunting-and-gathering expedition."

The speakers blared with what sounded like a trembling cymbal. Next, a mellow back-beat kicked in followed by a sampling of female vocals. Finally, rapper LL Cool J began speaking about the kind of woman he wanted.

Bradley didn't care much for rap music, especially the newer stuff that had emerged. Too much of it sounded like was raw, babbling aggression spat in forced rhymes to rhythms lifted from other R&B tunes. It wasn't fun or particularly insightful or poetic. It was silly. The lyrics didn't speak to him in any meaningful way. It wasn't a part of his world nor did it satisfy any particular yearning. It seemed the one and only message was *Better step off, 'cause I'm pissed off.* He wasn't pissed off, generally speaking, and felt no compulsion to appreciate the so-called music of the streets made by *homeboyz* and *homegirlz* who seemingly lacked any semblance of home training.

But he liked this tune. It was catchy. Sure, LL's *Around the Way Girl* featured the bass refrain and chords from *All Night Long*, a mid

-tempo tune by the Mary Jane Girls. However, the bass line had been retooled, smoothing out some of the bumps to make it faster.

As LL began defining his ideal woman, Bradley noticed a faint ringing in the background. He hadn't heard it before. It was a dizzying, dreamy sound that one might hear if his head were spinning—as if falling in love. The ringing gave the song a subtle sexual tension that built slowly until its release when the male background vocals surged forth with "I need a'round the way girl." A lyrical accent from the original song completed the song's transformation. LL had turned the song on its head. Where the Mary Jane Girls sang about their desire to please their men all night long, LL Cool J explained he needed an independent woman, preferably one with a bad attitude who demands you meet her half way. It spoke to Bradley like no other rap song had.

James and Bradley had returned to the city for their night out. Bradley had suggested they check out Oasis, a club on the city's westside that catered to an older crowd, but James vetoed the idea, saying: "That's out. They've done the white-folks electric slide. You know, changed the format…Yup. They done gone country," he said in a honky-tonk drawl. "Yeah, I guess they figured there were just too many brothas starting to hang out there when they were doing the Top 40 thing."

"Yeah, well, I guess country music is a good way to get rid of the black folks."

"Word," said James, who then broke into song. *Oh, give me a home, where the brothas don't roam…"*

Bradley laughed while James continued a cappella:

> *…And the beer, you don't have to pay*
> *Where seldom is heard, a negritude word,*
> *And the skies are not cloudy all day.*

"Yeah, man," said James, "the only brotha you gonna see up in that motherfucker is Charlie Pride."

"Man,' Bradley laughed, "you're sick."

"They'll be back, though; just as soon as they remember that white folks don't like shit either. Not our white folks, at least." He chuckled.

James exited the freeway and made a left onto the avenue before continuing on toward the heart of the city to The Studio.

Traffic was light as James drove pass Ellington Manor standing guard on the edge of downtown. Bradley's neck craned sideways as he checked out the elegant six-story building whose front entrance was sheltered with a forest-green awning and lit with a pair of floodlights. The old Art-Deco structure maintained a welcoming presence at a time when much of downtown had become a monument to boarded-up storefronts, surface parking lots, and bad choices. Built in the 1920s when the city was on the rise, the Ellington stood on the avenue in all its grandeur, like a lonely romantic from an era lost.

"I've always loved that old building," said Bradley, lost in reverie.

James glanced quickly at the relic but remained silent.

"Ever been inside?" Bradley asked.

"Nope…You?"

"Yeah, once…There was this woman I knew who lived there."

"White babe?"

Bradley chuckled. "Yeah."

She was a pretty young woman, not long out of a sorority house at the University of Michigan. A young metallurgist, she worked in research and development at Delcorp; one of several departmental stops Bradley had made as a high school co-opt student. Donna was her name, and she'd requested his services for a little assignment. (Co-opts were routinely shared among the department staff who had gofer tasks that needed doing.) Oddly enough, Bradley had seen her a week or so earlier at Highland Appliance where he had brought his weekly earnings to buy a Technics turntable. "So this is what you do with all your money," she'd said. "Well, Technics is good." She smiled approvingly.

Donna needed a piece of three-quarter-inch diameter iron cut to run some tests for a new spark plug shell. Bradley, as always, eagerly accepted the task.

The coil was outside. She led him out into the scrap yard where under a bright and unforgiving sun, he'd loosened his necktie and hack-sawed a two-foot section of rod. She was very grateful and the perspiring future engineer said, "you're welcome."

The next time she saw Bradley, she asked if he was interested in another task—a freelance job for which he would be paid. Sure, he said. *Moving a half-dozen boxes or so downstairs to a storage closet in the basement at Ellington Manor?* "No problem," he said.

After hauling the boxes of books and knick-knacks to the elevator for a trip to the basement—a job she could have done herself, he would think later—and rearranging a few pieces of furniture, she offered him a beer. Sure, he allowed, not so much because he wanted it, but because he was fearful of appearing ungrateful or inexperienced.

She handed him a sweaty, green bottle of Heineken. He sipped the beer cautiously. He panned the room, taking note of hardwood floors, the bay window, and the charming, dark-wood French doors that separated the living room from the small dining area.

The room's character set off remembrances of his architectural dream books. He swallowed more beer.

Meanwhile, she launched into his private affairs. *What college are you going to? Majoring in engineering? What do your parents do? Are you the first one in your family to attend college? Why not go away to school? How do you like working at Delcorp? What do you think of your supervisor? What do you want most out of life? You seem very serious. What's your girlfriend's name? What? A handsome guy like you doesn't have a girlfriend?*

Bradley sipped, nodded, smiled, and answered each question dutifully. The alcohol jabbed away at his brain until he felt a little punch drunk.

She was nice and pretty. He was captivated by the way she tried to put him at ease against his own nature. She respected his ideas and the liked the way he carried himself. She'd often remarked how well he dressed at work, and once suggested, he hold a class for some of the older guys in the department.

But at that moment, while seated in a director's chair across from her as she sat on the sofa, Bradley was most taken by the way her precious, unadorned lips came together and puckered when she drank from the bottle. He wanted to kiss those lips. Nursing a cold, damp bottle of beer while blood converged in his crotch, he wondered if she thought as much of his lips.

The shy seventeen-year-old kid left with twenty dollars and a hard dick to keep him company on the bike ride home. It was then it occurred to Bradley that maybe he was supposed to step up and lead *her*. He was supposed to be the man.

"Oh, wait," said James, his memory jogged. "Are you talking about that white chick from way back in the day?" He grinned.

"Yeah."

"Man, you should have hit that. Shit! You realize how that would have looked on your resume?"

The brothers laughed.

"Yeah, maybe so," said Bradley. "Too much of a young gentleman, I suppose."

"Yeah," James chimed in, "and then you grew up and realized that ladies want it just as much as us gentlemen. And, sometimes, even more."

The line outside The Studio on the Main Street was mostly white people in preppy attire. Bradley would fit right in, dressed in his white shirt, cable tennis sleeveless pullover, khakis, and loafers.

Meanwhile, the clientele inside ranged in age from upper college classmen to a post-collegiate demographic. The set was a bit on the young side for either brother but it was a start.

A doorman was checking IDs for the twenty-one and older entrance requirement, although underage whites were admitted routinely. Few blacks were ever cut any slack. Those that were usually moved in the safe company of whites. But two or more underage blacks, minus any white co-signers, could forget it.

After parking, the brothers made their way to the line.

"So finish telling me about this new honey of yours, Clare," said Bradley.

"Oh, man. She's tight. Works out and shit. Lots of style. Yeah, she works in marketing at the bank downtown. They're doing a new campaign. That's how we hooked up. Man, the first time I hit that, I was so aroused. I was like, 'whoa, this will be over in a matter of seconds, if I'm not careful.' And you know brothas—we gotta make that good first impression. But, man, I'm here to tell ya. That shit felt so good, I was about to cry."

Bradley was still laughing when they took their place behind a group of young white women who were coatless as were many of their cohorts in the subfreezing night air.

"Man, James, you're a ho."

"No I'm not. I just love to love my sistas."

"Dang, man. You make it sound so, so incestuous."

"Yeah, well, whatever. I just want my sistas to know that I'm here for 'em."

They laughed and tapped fists.

"Can I see some IDs, gents?" the doorman asked.

The brothers detected sarcasm and they shot quick glances at each other while retrieving their wallets. Though neither man looked under twenty-one, it didn't stop the doorman from closely examining their driver licenses. He looked at Bradley's ID and Bradley as if to make sure the two matched. He handed it back to him.

"The guy in this picture has a mustache and goatee," he said to James.

"And now I don't," James replied, reaching for his license. "Now you see it; now you don't."

The doorman said nothing but handed over the plastic-laminated card.

"I didn't hear you ask the Bangles for any ID," said James. He knew the routine and disliked it just the same. "And they looked all of eighteen too."

"Just doing my job, chief. That's all."

"Yeah let me guess, you know them. I could tell how chummy all you guys were."

The brothers entered the club and headed straight for the bar. Along the way, Bradley joked that perhaps he should have told the doorman he met the HIV-positive athlete America says it loves so dearly.

"That wouldn't have mattered," said James, still perturbed. "He probably would have tried to blame you for giving the brotha HIV."

They each downed a shot of Tequila before cleansing their palates and throats with a couple of Heinekens. They explored the club, its lower and upper floors, looking for no one in particular. They watched the overwhelmingly white revelers dance, including a small group of women who seemed to be having a ball together. But they left the club less than an hour after arriving. For James, The Studio was merely a tune-up stop and a place to possibly see a familiar face or two.

Bradley was just along for the ride.

They finished their brews and headed for the door. Outside, the doorman was still guarding the entrance.

"See you next time, chief," James said.

"I'll be here."

"Yeah, I'm sure you will," said James, who always had to have the last word.

They drove north up Main Street. They passed by one of the more recent downtown rescue missions, a festival marketplace located just south of the river.

"Man, what was the name of that restaurant that used to be in the Pavilion?" James asked.

"Oh, I know which one you're thinking of, but I can't think of the name right now."

"Anyway, I wasn't sad to see that place go. No sir-ee. You remember that time we rolled in there and they were checking IDs at the door."

"Yeah."

"After proving we were twenty-one to get into the place, the bartender carded us again. I asked the dude why it was necessary to show ID a second time since you had to be twenty-one to get in this motherfucking place. Then this mug wants to cop an attitude."

"Yeah. And then you rammed your license at his face, stopping about an inch from his nose," said Bradley, chuckling as he recalled the scene. "He was like, 'Hey, buddy. Hey, buddy. Take it easy. Take it easy.'"

"Shit, dude asked to the see my license. I was just trying to make it easy for him. And you were like, 'Cool out, James. Relax.'... Yeah, the second time that shit happened I was with Pam," said James, his voice devoid of all playfulness. "It was the same old bullshit. They card us at the door and we go in and have a seat. Then the waitress came over and wanted to see some ID So, you know, me, B. I politely asked,

'Don't you have to be twenty-one to get in this motherfucker?' I mean, I didn't say 'motherfucker', but you know what I'm saying."

"Right."

"Then the white ho says, 'Look, if you want to drink in here, you're going to have to show me some ID.' And then the bitch stormed off."

"I don't think you've told me this before."

"Really? Shit yeah, man."

"So, what did you do?"

"Oh, we were pissed. Pam was ready to get off in old girl's ass. But I was like, nope. Nope, let's speak to the manager. Let's handle this the proper way. He came over and we explained the deal and how the waitress got all indignant and shit. Then *this* motherfucker—oh, he was a big white boy, too. I guess I was supposed to be scared. I was like: *motherfucker, I'm a trained killer. You don't scare me. I will fuck you up.* Anyway, dude had the balls to say, 'Well, maybe you were the ones who got hostile.' I said, 'Excuse me? *What?*' I couldn't believe what I'd just heard. Man, I wanted to beat his white ass; beat his motherfucking ass right there. So we left, man. We left. And I never went back, which is probably what they wanted anyway. Right?"

The older brother was silent for a moment. He then asked, "You think maybe the waitress was mad or uncomfortable because she had to do something that she knew was wrong and didn't want to do?"

"You mean like being told to hassle the black customers?"

"Yeah."

"I dunno. Maybe. Maybe not." James was momentarily contemplative. "Anyway, when I heard they were closing their doors, I said, 'Good. That's what you motherfuckers get.'"

James turned up the music.

They were silent as the landscape continued to change. The car motored pass a big, old empty shell of a building that was the Parker Hotel—once the city's finest—and yet another large and ever-desolate parking lot. Meanwhile, Public Enemy's *Shut 'Em Down* coloured the background.

"You know," James began, as he lowered the volume again.

Bradley turned and saw his brother's concentrated stare, as if he weren't negotiating his way through the slight traffic on Main Street but traveling a far different and anfractuous route.

"I actually considered calling the state civil rights commission, the N-double-A or somebody after that last incident. Yup, I sure did," he added, as if the world doubted him.

"You mean at that restaurant?"

"Yeah, man. I almost did it. But then I just said, 'Skip it. What's the use?' You know?"

Bradley was silent.

The Riviera Lounge, or "the Rivvy," as it was known, was an after-hours joint on the city's northside not too far from the massive Buick complex. Located on north Main Street, the Rivvy's neighbourhood was a bustling commercial district decades ago. That was when the street was lined with stores and shops that served the nearby neighbourhoods.

The area's character had changed long ago, set in motion by a complex array of circumstances. Some folks pointed to the open housing ordinance that passed narrowly by citywide referendum in late 1960s as the beginning of the end.

Small businesses and shops that once anchored the area had given way to the occasional fast-food restaurant franchise or rib crib, beer, and wine stores with bright, billboard signs screaming *LIQUOR SOLD HERE, LOTTERY, CHECKING CASHING, MONEY ORDERS and WIC COUPONS ACCEPTED*. There also were other dingy little establishments that passed themselves off as "social clubs."

Then there was the Riviera Lounge.

Compared to the other after-hours joints and social clubs, the Rivvy was halfway respectable. The establishment at least tried to appear 100-percent legitimate even if a beer, a shot of Hennessy, or a Seagram's wine cooler could all be bought there well after 2 a.m.—when legal liquor sales ended. The owners also considered its patrons peace of mind by providing good security.

The small parking adjacent to the club was filled with an array of shiny American-made sedans, but mostly GM. Parked near the entrance was a squat, pit bull of a vehicle—a silver Geo Tracker with tinted windows, sparkling rims, and narrow-sidewall tires. The north and southbound sides of Main Street near the club were lined with more cars.

James found an open space along Main Street just north of the club. Although the spot was perhaps a bit closer, he passed up parking on a dark side street just south of the club, saying, as if thinking aloud:

"Fuck *that*. I ain't getting my ass robbed tonight by Jimmy the Crackhead."

When Bradley joked he had his brother's back, James replied, "Not unless you're packing a Nine, bruh."

Small bands of men and women made their way to the Rivvy's side door entrance where a jumbled line snaked backwards toward the parking lot like a soup line. A few were professionally attired like they were going to work at an investment house or law firm. Others had a gaudy elegance about them. And some were plain tacky. One man, wearing an open-collar eggshell coloured silk shirt, even attached a boutonniere on the lapel of his brown suit with white pinstripes. Most, however, were dressed somewhere along the lines of James. And no one's attire violated the "no blue jeans (which applied only to men); no gym shoes, no ball caps" dress code.

"How y'all brothas doin' tonight?" said the beefy doorman when the brothers stepped forward.

"I'm straight, dog, now," James replied.

"Good," said Bradley.

"Just need to pat y'all down."

James held his arms outward as if he were soaring in midair while the doorman frisked him for weapons. Bradley was next. He, too, held his arms outward and feigned nonchalance about the Rivvy's stop-and-frisk policy. The search gave him some peace of mind knowing anyone packing had to check his or her gun at the door. It was, however, deeply troubling on another level. *So it's really come to this*, he thought.

"Y'all have a good night," the doorman said before repeating his routine with the next group of patrons.

Bradley followed James up the narrow corridor as the music's roar and echo surged like the sound of an ocean tucked just behind a grassy knoll. Striding down the dimly lit, wood-paneled hallway with its low, drop ceiling, he felt crowded and unsure of his surroundings.

He could count on three fingers the number of times he had been to the Riviera Lounge. It wasn't anywhere he would go with Abby for a night on the town. The place seemed like a firetrap. It reminded him of driving through the Detroit-Windsor tunnel. Although, as an engineer, he trusted the science on which the tunnel was built, the trip beneath the cold, dark waters of the Detroit River still had a tendency to unsnarl his kinky hair if the tunnel traffic moved too slow or came to a halt.

The sound of Stevie Wonder's *My Eyes Don't Cry* filled the club. A small team of women and two men were bulldozing the dance floor doing the electric slide. The line dance moved north, south, east, then west until the floor had been cleared several times over. The dancers rolled evenly back and forth and to and fro, with the fluid motion of water in a shaken basin. Their movements were synchronous, though a few dancers added flair to the simple routine by improvising on the steps like Miles' fingertips on a jazz standard. A visitor from another world might have thought they had rehearsed together.

"Ah, yes," James said. "The dance of the new black consciousness movement. Black folks are dancing together again."

Bradley shook his head and chuckled. "You don't quit."

"I'd die if I did."

The brothers worked their way to the long bar where a shapely dark-skinned sista took their drink orders. She wore her hair in a ponytail and adorned her lips with red lipstick. Her eyes had only a trace of mascara. The makeup accented her alluring features rather well, Bradley thought. Each ear, which had been pierced four times, was decorated with gold hoop earrings of descending size. The trinkets resembled a succession of fish each being gobbled up a larger one that followed.

As they waited their second Tequila shots and Heinekens to arrive, James caught a glimpse of a woman seated two stools away from them at the bar. Her posture indicated she was available for dancing and conversation, and maybe more. She had robust thighs and a head full of tiny braids that resembled a plate of black pasta.

James checked her out quickly before turning to his brother on the sly to croon: "On top of spaghetti..."

"That's messed up, J," Bradley snickered, after seeing what prompted the ditty.

She caught Bradley looking at her and rolled her eyes with

a "humph."

He, in turn, thought: *Yeah, she's a little thick, but I could work with it.*

Presently, the center of the room was flat and empty. The perimeter was filled with tables and chairs, most of which were occupied with sedate patrons. The lighting dazzled the patch of parquet tiling that made up the dance floor. The night was still fresh and energetic. A beacon of light perched upon a four-foot-tall speaker scrambled the darkness.

People continued to trickle inside and movement through the isles became more difficult. The music was pumping and a few people found themselves on the dance floor. The brothas were checking out the sistas, and the sistas noticing the brothas.

Bradley lit a cigarette, his first since he and James had been out that evening.

"When did you start smoking again?" he asked.

"I only do it occasionally, mostly at work."

James nodded slowly but said nothing. He resumed surveying the crowd.

"All right, y'all," said DJ, from his corner perch across the room, "let's get this party started for real."

And in perfect timing, the speakers then blared:

HIT IT!

"Ooh." James popped off the bar rail. "That's ma' jam. Gotta go. Watch my drink."

He made his way to a nearby table where four women were seated. He extended his right hand to a caramel-coloured woman with large eyes and a show-stopping smile. James tilted his head twice quickly toward the dance floor with a mock bashfulness.

She nodded affirmatively and stood up. She was fine, Bradley thought, and the kind of woman he never had much luck with. Tall and lean, dressed in black leather slacks, her hair looked as though she had spent all afternoon at the salon. A female version of a fade, her hairdo featured large, fuller curls on top with progressively smaller, micro-mini curls on the sides.

The driving bass lifted others from their seats as well. A female voice began to explain the obvious—that it took two to make things go right—as the dance floor disappeared underneath the scores of dancing feet. The spaghetti lady accepted the extended hand of a man who then led her to the dance floor. The dance court was swollen with gyrating bodies, tangled arms, and bobbing heads all moving in rhythm.

The music played on without Bradley. He instead leaned against the bar, which now had plenty of elbowroom, with his Heineken and cigarette to keep him company. Earlier that evening, he joked about how he hadn't "danced competitively in a while." Nowadays his dancing was limited largely to doing the two-step in the living room with Abby while Sarah Vaughn serenaded them with *Embraceable You*. But he had never been much for dance clubs, anyway. He wasn't much of a dancer. It made him self-conscious to think so many eyes might be watching him.

He wondered at times whether it was his lack of real dance skills—something that had been missing in his social repertoire—that made it so difficult to meet women in such places. Watching from afar as his brother and others worked to the music, he felt a certain estrangement from the group; the way a married person might feel when they've spent too much time with their in-laws at the expense of their own family gatherings.

It was funny, he thought, recalling the differences between dancing in a room full of white folks and one filled with blacks. The expectations, that is. Black folks simply expected you to get up and move something. Join the party. Slow jams were a little different only because the woman didn't want you out there embarrassing her by dancing off beat, especially if there wasn't much of a crowd on the dance floor to get lost among.

But in white gatherings, he noticed some folks tended to watch him like he was an NBA star playing a pick-up game at a country club. Every move he made was treated with an air of authenticity and esteem, like they thought he could really get down if he wanted to. Like he was an MC Hammer in their midst.

Even the one white guy at those gatherings, who'd swear he could jam with the best of them and was determined to prove it, gave him too much respect. So Bradley thought nothing of basking in that royal glow while it lasted. *Hell, why not?*

Black folks knew the deal, though. They could tell the real dancers from those like himself, who could merely or barely keep a beat and not embarrass himself.

Bradley sucked again on his cigarette and exhaled. He rinsed his mouth with a swig of beer before chuckling at the silliness of it all. He then promised himself he'd get up and join the party on the next jam.

It was well after midnight when he returned to his house in the suburbs. James assured his older brother he was okay to drive home and didn't need to crash in the guest room this time. He thought about calling Abby to answer the question she'd left hours earlier on the answering machine: "Honey, where are you?" But he decided against it. The hour was late, and she was probably asleep.

He instead reached for the phone number on the dresser; the one belonging to Luscious. Carefully, he punched in the digits and waited for her to answer his call. The alcohol running in his veins helped alleviate the anxiety he would have felt otherwise. The voice he soon heard was a tape-recording of the one he'd conversed with in person the previous night.

"This is Bradley," he said, his voice low and furtive. "You know? The engineer with a little imagination?" He chuckled. "I'll try you again later. Bye-bye."

Click.

Friday

But God bless the child that's got his own

18

At five o'clock in the morning, the clock radio arrested him from a deep slumber. He reached over quietly and gently touched the device in just the right spot to silence it. He slipped back into sleep until he heard another cut from the soundtrack of his dreams. Finally, after smacking the chatterbox a third time for its persistent mouthiness, he decided he'd had enough. He turned off the alarm.

He pushed back the comforter and staggered to the bathroom to pee. The cold ceramic tile against his bare feet made him shiver and caused his sphincters to tighten as his bladder emptied. His reflection in the mirror looked pissed as the bright artificial light made him frown and squint.

He felt sickly, unrested and a little unsteady. He braced himself with his free hand against the wall. Once his trickling penis dripped no more, he snapped his briefs back into place and stumbled back into the bedroom. He plunged back into the queen-sized bed, submersing himself in its warmth.

Friday, he decided right then and there was a good—no, a great day—to sleep late. He grabbed the telephone off the nightstand and placed a gravelly-voiced call to his supervisor's answering machine to alert to him that he would be making it a three-day weekend. He had already planned on working just a half-day, which had been scheduled well before he and Gary completed a productive Thursday debugging the new line, and before he realized he'd be out well past his bedtime the night before. Now, toss in a mild hangover, a few hours of sleep, and another cold, overcast morning, it was a prescription for a full day's rest. Delcorp would have to make spark plugs without him.

He reawakened a couple of hours later better than he was before. His former self hadn't returned completely, but his head throbbed less and his stance was more firm. Not having to rush outside into the cold pleased him immensely.

His pace was leisurely as he retrieved the morning paper. A winter-like grayness blanketed the subdivision. All chimneys poking through the rooftops huffed and puffed like tiny smokestacks.

At the snack counter, he drank coffee while reading the morning's top story and listening to the same one discussed on the *Today Show*. The shock of yesterday's news had worn off somewhat. Now came all the reaction and analysis by expert and amateur alike.

> *"I'm stunned, absolutely stunned. It's like a good friend or someone in your family falling ill."*
>
> . . .
>
> *"I'll be praying for him and his family. He's one of our few black men that America seems to truly love. Oh, and that smile. We'd sure hate to lose him."*
>
> . . .
>
> *"He's a winner, no doubt; a great role model; a great competitor."*
>
> . . .
>
> *"Boy, if it can happen to someone like him."*

The comments were those of four people in Miami there for a conference on diversity training, the article explained. He was certain it was Abby's contribution, the wire story the *Daily News* had published in response to what appeared to be a national tragedy.

Seeing her name in print reminded him he hadn't spoken to her since early yesterday. He picked up the phone and started dialing.

"Good morning, Ace."

"Good morning to you," Abby replied. "I was just about to call you as soon as I finished packing. Say, where were you last night? I called."

"Yeah, I got your message. I got in late and I didn't want to wake you."

"Where did you go?"

"James came by and made me go out with him."

"Made you?"

"Yeah," he chuckled. "We didn't get in 'til sometime after midnight."

"Midnight? Wait a minute, where are you now?"

"Home."

"I thought it seemed awfully quiet in the background. What did you guys do?"

"Bar hopping. We stopped at The Studio."

"The Studio?"

"Yeah, it was senior citizen's night," he said, in place of the actual name for the Thursday night soiree, 'college night. "Then we drove up to the Rivera Lounge. You know, the after-hours joint up on north Main."

"Mm-hmm."

"I was so tired and a little hung-over this morning, I just decided to take the day off."

The line went quiet.

"So did you guys pick up any women last night?"

"C'mon."

"I know how James is. He's always out tomcatting around."

"No he isn't. "Okay, well, maybe a little bit. But he says he's found someone special. They've even talked about inviting us over for dinner."

"Oh, really. So James has found the woman of his dreams?"

"Well, those weren't his exact words," he chuckled. "But he says he really likes her. So, anyway, I told him to let us know when dinner will be ready. Hey, I saw your stuff in the paper this morning," said Bradley, lifting up the newspaper.

"What does it say?"

"Looks like they used four people you interviewed in a story." He read the quotes and the summary paragraph to her. "Also, your name is at the end of the article."

"Oh, they gave me tagline. Well, that's okay. At least we got something in. It's a huge story."

"Yeah, that's all they're talking about on the *Today Show* this morning."

"Anyway, like I said, I decided to take the whole day off to recuperate."

The couple paused.

"Hey, I really am sorry about going off on you the other day about the article and all. The week just got off to a very bad start, I guess. You're not here. You're far away. It's cold. And then there's work, where I'm treated to the story of the happy black hobo. And..." his voice trailed off.

"Yeah, I know. Those guys, ugh. Listen, sweetheart, I need to finish packing and get down stairs. Don't forget about this afternoon."

"I won't. Have a good flight, by the way."

"Ha. Ha. Very funny."

"No, really. I mean it. Just sit back and relax, and I'll see you this afternoon. Everything will be fine."

After an exchange of "I love you," Bradley got off the phone, made himself a western omelet, and sat down to finish the paper. The county prosecutor had scheduled a news conference Monday morning to discuss the case of the victim-turned-outlaw, according to one article. Another explained a verdict was possible today in the case of three men charged with dangling a scarecrow onto the interstate at night that resulted in the death of a motorist who swerved to miss it. All of that and now the star athlete who announced he has the AIDS virus.

In another section he saw an ad for *Tie me up! Tie me down!*. It was showing at the art institute theatre Friday and Saturday evening. With Abby home, he thought about dinner and an artsy movie. And maybe a stop by Lucy's afterwards? Maybe.

He spent the remainder of the morning cleaning up the house in preparation for his fiancée's return. The dishes he washed by hand because there weren't enough to justify loading the dishwasher.

Elsewhere, clean towels were added in the master bathroom. The bed linens were changed too. So fresh did the replacement sheets feel and smell that he briefly entertained the notion of diving back into bed for a pampered nap. He resisted the impulse, concluding the mere thought of an idea is sometimes far more satisfying than its reality.

He instead gathered up the used linen and headed downstairs to start the washer. A small napkin on the dresser was folded neatly and tucked away in a recess of his wallet.

The mindless chores were therapeutic and helped suppress

feelings of guilt, which had begun to set in. He realized he could have gone to work today day after all. Later that afternoon, he made several work-related phone calls to further ease his conscience before throwing on a pair of blue jeans, a hooded sweatshirt, and black Nike Air Jordans. He grabbed his brown bomber jacket and headed out the door into the blustery air. Large snowflakes swirled about, the ground peppered.

After stops at the Post Office and dry cleaners, he made his way over to the northside for some sweet potato pie. It had become one of Abby's favourite desserts. She thought it tasted like pumpkin pie but sweeter and better, and he knew of a place that made it well. It was a soul-food kitchen located in a crumbing part of town next to a party store. The store's unfriendly clerks with attitudes sold cigarettes, beer and wine, formula, lottery tickets, and dream books from behind a wall of Plexiglas an inch thick. Outside, the building resembled a NASCAR racer for all the tobacco and other ads plastered on it.

The restaurant was cramped and surprisingly pleasant, even though the rib and chicken dinners were just okay. The chicken was better. It was the sweet potato pie that brought him back time and again, and the owner always let him know how much he appreciated the patronage. He placed three slices of pie into a brown paper sack and tossed in a few napkins and several plastic forks, as if he thought the treats might be eaten somewhere other than home. Outside, just as Bradley was about to slip into his car, he noticed a man with his hands stuffed into his pockets coming his way. He wore an oversized, red hooded sweatshirt underneath a down vest-jacket, somewhat baggy pants, and gym shoes that fit like hiking boots. He looked like Little Red Riding Hood metamorphosed into the Grim Reaper.

19

Abby's plane was late, and the delay only gave her more time to think dreadful thoughts about flying. Why was it late? Was there a mechanical problem? If so, did they really fix it? How did they know the problem wouldn't resurface at the worst possible time? Because they were running late, would the pilots then be rushed to make up lost time by skimping on the pre-flight procedures, even at the risk of safety? Maybe there was a crash. If so, what were odds of another airline disaster occurring on the same day? What would the front-page look like? Thousands of flights take-off and land safely each day. Would hers be the odd one that didn't? She glanced out the windows at gate A5. Still, no plane. The A5 steel door leading to the accordion tunnel was shut. She wished to be home with Bradley.

Abby took to studying the faces of those around her. Casually, she looked at each face in her gate area, taking mental notes and wondered if she could describe them should disaster strike and she survived. There were children, old people, students, and business types. White people. Black people. Hispanics and Asians. Were these the faces of tragedy? How it is that their fates should become linked?

Still, no airplane. They would be late arriving in St. Louis, which pointed to another problem with this town—few direct flights to destination spots. That meant plane changes, possible extended layovers, and double the anxiety associated with extra take-offs and landings. Worst yet, Bradley told her snow was expected Friday and Saturday. So the landing could be bumpy. At least the sun was finally shining in Miami.

"Abigail Larsen. What are you doing here in Miami?"

Surprised, Abby's head shifted quickly in the direction from which that vaguely familiar voice came.

"Michael? Michael Bellamy?" She rose up.

"It's me."

The two hugged. He planted a soft kiss on her cheek, which took her aback.

"How are you? It's been a long time. I barely even recognized you. But when you said Abigail, I knew it had to be you."

"Yeah, well, I remember how much you liked being called Abigail." He grinned slyly. "So how are you? You look great. I mean, really."

"Thank you. Well, you've certainly changed. Look at your hair."

Gone was the wavy-top, low fade of yesteryear. This new man wore baby dreadlocks, three-day beard, and an earring. He still smelled very nice, but clearly there had been some changes since the days of Philosophy 101.

"Yeah, well, you haven't changed much; still look the same. Still as lovely as always."

She smiled, thinking some things, however, never change. "Where are you headed? Traveling for work?"

"Well, you know I'm with the Herald now."

"Oh, that's right. Covering sports, right?"

"Uh-huh. Yup. Doing a little feature writing, too. So where are you these days?"

"The *Daily News*."

"Really?"

"Mm-hmm. Yeah, I'm covering local politics and county government."

The old lovers paused briefly and just sort of looked each other over.

"Wow. It's really great to see you. You're looking good. And that's a nice rock on your finger there. Married?"

"Engaged."

"Okay. When's the date?"

"Haven't set one yet. Sometime next year, though, summer, early fall."

"Anyone I know?"

"No I don't think so."

"Okay." He folded his arms across his chest. "Man."

"What about you?"

"Still looking. Correction: I'm not really looking. I guess I'm not in any hurry."

She nodded. Somehow that wasn't surprising, she thought. "So how do you like the *Herald?* Boy, you're big time."

"I don't know about all that. But it's okay. It's a job, you know? I'm just getting back from an assignment. I do a fair amount of traveling. I do like that, I guess," he said. "So what brings you to Miami?"

"I was here for work."

"What? On assignment or something?"

"Sort of. I attended a conference on diversity in the workplace."

"Okay."

"I'm on my way back now. My flight is running late."

"Oh, that's too bad. If you were going to be here, I was going to see if you were free for dinner or something."

"Sorry. Some other time, I guess."

"Oh, while I'm thinking about it: Here, let me give you a card." He reached for his wallet.

"I'm sorry I don't have any with me."

"That's all right. Here you go." He placed the card in her hand. He again folded his arms and resumed staring down at her from his imaginary perch. A computer satchel hung from his shoulder. Abby studied the card briefly before placing it in her purse.

"So do you get back to Michigan much?"

"I try to get home several times a year. My father has been ill recently. I was home about two months ago when he had surgery. He has prostate cancer, but I think they got it all."

"Is he going to be okay?"

"I think so. The doctors say they caught it early. But we'll have to wait to see."

"Well, I wish you and your family all the best."

"Thank you very much. He's a tough old dude, though."

Michael paused and looked Abigail over once more before saying, "Abigail Larsen. I'll be damned."

Abby smiled momentarily as she fixed her eyes on the dimple in his right cheek, visible even through close-cropped facial hair. He was still quite handsome, in a whole new way, and confident as ever. Abby's memory scrolled.

"You know," she said, "I saw an article of yours a while back. Yeah, the one you wrote for *Essence*."

His eyes widened as his expression begged for more information before he remembered the one. "Oh really? *Really?*" His lips pursed as his head yielded a slow nod of affirmation. "Okay."

"Yeah. Interesting piece."

"Oh, well, thank you. I was, well, um…" He dropped his arms and took a step back. His thumbs found the corners of his trouser pockets and he looked like a reluctant gunslinger preparing to draw.

It had been a long time since the two had shared intimacies. So long, in fact, it almost seemed as though it never really happened. And yet it did. He had written of his foray in interracial romance as something of a youthful indiscretion. Seemingly begging for forgiveness, Michael wrote that white womanhood and sexuality so thoroughly dominated the mainstream American male psyche that it became an almost must-have item—a commodity, if you will—for all men of means, regardless of race, colour, creed or national origin. As though that's all there was, if you ever watched television, read any men's magazines, or paid any attention at all to advertising.

Michael had written that white femininity—like all good fantasies, it seemed—was crafted to satisfy a particular yearning for young, horny brothas, which in this case was uninhibited sexual fulfillment. That is, they were sexually liberated in a way the typical black girl was not. An openness that was said to manifest itself, for the most part:

> *…in their willingness to participate in oral sex more readily than the kind of sista a brotha might want to marry someday.*

Black women, in contrast, as enthralling sexual beings barely existed (if at all) in the eyes of so-called mainstream America, he asserted in print. It certainly seemed to have no place outside the black community which, as a definable entity, was getting smaller and smaller and smaller. The article further stated:

> *But, in an odd way, contemporary black sistas were more fortunate than their white sistas in some ways. Side-by-side with all else being equal—class status and the like—white men seem more deferential toward black women. Black men, too. Black women, it seemed, exuded something uncommonly strong that cautioned one that he'd best mind his manners.*

As a college student, Michael had written, he saw himself as someone who one day would be very successful in some field other than civil rights activism. It was, after all, a new day. Moreover, he not only wanted to see what all the fuss was about when it came to white babes, he deemed it an important part of his overall education, not unlike learning how to play golf for the executive trainee.

> *You either had to buy into certain conventions, or you had to disassociate yourself almost entirely from a large chunk of Americana.*

Michael wrote that he had bought into the fantasy and thus wanted to know what he was getting for his money.

Abby stood silent and confident in her belief that Michael figured he'd never have to answer for that piece to someone face-to-face who mattered. Whether there had been others, she didn't know or care. But certainly she must've provided him with some material. He had as much right to analyze his life experiences as anyone else. *Right?* If he chose to write about those experiences, well, that was his business, too. *Turnabout is fair play for the journalist, right?*

But something didn't feel right for her. To be looked upon and treated in that way—as a sampling, or sorts—when there were so many white women who were nothing at all like her, wasn't cool.

"Ok. So, I gotta ask," Michael said. "What did you think when you read it? Did you think it was about you? Were you offended at all?"

I'm not some kind of guinea pig, she wanted to say; nor the embodiment of some mythical creature you wish to love, loath, or possess.

"Umm," Abby said. "Well, you didn't mention me by name or anything, so it's not like I was misquoted. It was strange, though, seeing your byline and recalling those days. Let's just say that I have a different memory of that time."

"Yeah, well, I guess it was, I don't know, therapeutic, I guess."

"Wait. Did you say, *therapeutic?*"

He grinned, sheepishly. "Probably not the best choice of words."

"Oh, I dunno." She paused and then chuckled. "Sure it wasn't just a byline that you were collecting?"

He paused as though considering the assessment, chuckled softly, and then shrugged. Abby was silent.

"Maybe so," he said after a moment of reflection. "I am trying to do more freelance work," he said, trying to shift the topic.

"Really? Well, good for you. Good luck with that," she said. "But maybe leave me out of it the next time, huh?"

Michael chuckled uncomfortably while Abby's smile was tight-lipped. After an exchange of best wishes, he said he needed to run. They hugged once more—with less affection than before—and parted ways. Abby resumed the wait for her ride home and thought, *what an asshole.* And that was that.

20

Flight 1310 finally docked and a stream of passengers flooded out of the gate. Abby felt her pulse quicken. When the airplane, reloaded with passengers, peanuts, and fuel, pushed away from the end of the accordion tunnel, she took a deep breath and wondered whether a single, panic-stricken passenger could force a plane to return to the gate. Not likely, she figured.

Once the aircraft leaped into the sky and the cabinet floor leveled off, she was determined not to spend her time counting the invisible air miles or watching the flight attendants wrestle with those awkward, stainless-steel lunchboxes on wheels.

From her perch high above the clouds, she decided there wasn't much else to ruminate over about the chance reunion with an old lover. That chapter was over.

She instead looked to the future and forced herself to concentrate on work. What was there to say about the weeklong diversity seminar?

She was at a loss to articulate her true feelings on the evaluation form Walter Montgomery & Associates' had asked them to complete during a wrap-up session earlier that day. Nor was she so inclined to write something profound the consultants might want to use as a lift-out quote on their brochure. Her thoughts at that time lay elsewhere, mainly on her afternoon flight.

She didn't have any ideas on how the course might be improved, so she left that space on the appraisal form blank. Under the section heading, Other Comments, she considered writing diversity training is the wrong medicine prescribed for all the right reasons before deciding against it.

Instead, she noted how odd it seemed the workshop didn't feature more female speakers. But as to her overall impressions, she merely jotted down a few vague comments saying it was interesting and worthwhile.

She felt the workshop was interesting in some respects, though probably not so much in the way the organizers had planned. That professional athlete's stunning disclosure a day earlier had the effect of placing the participants on the same plane much more so than any of the largely canned and regurgitated presentations. That single news event got people talking, and thinking about their own lives and their connection to others in a genuine way.

Why must something terrible happen before people bond? Still, aside from being part of a rather diverse group of people when the celebrity made his oddly serendipitous revelation, she could easily argue the training wasn't very useful.

However well intended, it would be naive to think such a seminar would provide some kind of religious epiphany or instantaneous transformation. In her mind, such a conversion would be as dubious as the behavior of that man she observed worshipping at a Pentecostal church while covering a story.

Abby had found herself at the church as a tag-along with a local judge who was campaigning for re-election. In black church after black church, the candidate gave the same speech almost verbatim. So having heard it all before, Abby spent her time watching the large congregation in what had been a spirited service.

She fixed her eyes on a man sitting in the pew across from hers. He appeared lost in some kind of trance until the pastor stepped forward and asked for the congregation to come forward with more tithing. The man suddenly awakened from his hypnotic state and rushed to the front of the church with a twenty-dollar bill in hand.

Oh, brother, she thought at the time. What a scam.

But then as she replayed the experience, she remembered how neither she nor Bradley were religious people and how that was her first and only visit to that church.

So what she interpreted as a phony meditative state may have well been something else that couldn't be fathomed in a single visit and a few observations. Moreover, she allowed that what's true of another person's experience mustn't necessarily be true of hers. That being the case, if that manner of worship helped make the man a better person, who was she to pass judgment?

The question the diversity seminar sought to address was how we can become better people in dealing with those of a different race or culture. She now felt a responsibility, if not to Walter Montgomery & Associates, then certainly to the Daily News editor, to provide some kind of thoughtful response.

Abby took out a pen and notebook and began to write.

For the average person, dealing with a person of another race is like the typical newspaper reader who doesn't want to take time to read thirty-five inches of copy. They want everything to fit inside of an inverted pyramid. Everything they think they need to know ought to be in the story's first few paragraphs. And if not there, then summarized in a chart.

She continued:

But you've got to give up something of yourself, like time. Give a moment of your time and figure out what's going on. 'Training is a process, not a single event.'

She wrote, paraphrasing the words of one of the instructors.

So, too, is getting to know someone of another race or culture. Oftentimes, we don't want to do that. We don't take the time to read the whole story, much less understand it. Cultural influences and family background certainly play a role in a person's development, but it doesn't define the whole person. The trick is learning to understand the influences and knowing which ones really do matter to that person, if at all. That only comes with time —

She paused a moment then continued.

And contact, if possible. Respect a person's individuality and allow them to be who they are. Also, recognize the complexity inherent in all relationships.

That's what the seminar lacked as it droned on about cultural traits and archetypes.

She wrote the preceding sentence in parentheses.

However, it seems only the most courageous dare cross the great divide when it comes to race, particularly when talking about blacks and whites. For everyone else, it's easy to fall back into the comfort zone of one's own race and

She stopped writing. *Courageous?* Was she talking about herself? She didn't feel so brave in any extraordinary sense. Abby really believed she just happened to fall in love with Bradley, who just happened to be black. Maybe the conditions were just right. But isn't that always the case? They had something in common and something to build upon.

Whatever it was, something between them just clicked. But just because she was engaged to a black man didn't make her immune to all things seemingly black and white. She knew that despite the frowns and raised eyebrows she encountered among his family, on the whole, they had been much more welcoming of her than her people had been of him.

Moreover, she still found some black men intimidating and knew of some black neighbourhoods she wouldn't likely jog through by herself, if at all. On the other hand, hadn't she visited more than one white neighbourhood, more than one trailer park, more than one tavern she found to be rather unpleasant, too? And if not for her necessarily, then certainly for Bradley or a black woman? White men could be intimidating as well in that disarmingly domineering sort of way. Before you knew it, he'd have his hand up your dress or be calling you *a dumb cunt* if you couldn't appreciate the way he came on to you. Before long, the questions would be reversed as he demanded: *Hey, what' s wrong with you?*

Strangely, however uneasy she felt around some black men, it wasn't often due to a real fear of being assaulted or something worse. Contrary to the cliché, she didn't feel the need to clutch her purse tighter whenever any ol' black man came near—and frankly, she had grown a bit weary of that same old story. No, this uneasiness grew out of a fear of the unknown in that perhaps you were dealing with an otherwise sane person whose wick was extremely short. It came packaged in a face and posture that said, just stay the fuck away from me. In those situations, she felt a need to watch herself more than usual. That is, she couldn't relax. She couldn't be herself. She felt unwelcomed.

She even saw the look occasionally in Bradley's face. But instead of anger, his look revealed itself in his amusement, or bemusement, perhaps. For at times around white strangers, he'd crack a smile that ran across his lips like a sparking fuse on a stick of dynamite.

It was a perceptive grin as if he were enjoying a private joke or engrossed in smoking a joint all by himself on the couch at a party. The look was so natural he didn't even seem to notice whenever it appeared. It was there and then it wasn't. Those experiences, however, weren't the sort one could easily put into words or discuss with a room full of diverse strangers.

So what now? She wondered.

Abby folded her hands on the tray table and looked out the window at the expansive splendor of the cottony, sun-drenched clouds below. The sight was breathtaking.

She mused, is this the view from Heaven?

21

Bradley saw the pigeon-toed man, dressed in his hooded sweatshirt, move closer. Before he could finish unlocking the car door and get inside, the man spoke through the swirling snow:

"Sup, dog," said a mildly fatigued voice from under the sweatshirt's hood.

"Hey, how's it going?"

The man frowned non-threateningly. "Ain't your name Bradley? Bradley Cunningham?"

"Yeah." Bradley was circumspect.

"You don't even remember me, do you?"

Bradley first frowned and then smiled upon recognizing the face of the former class clown.

"It's Marcus, man," the man said before Bradley could answer.

"Dang, man. How are you doing?"

The two men locked hands like true soul brothers.

"Oh, man. I'm straight. You know? Just on my way, to the J-O-B."

"Okay."

"Yeah. I saw you 'bout to get in your ride, and thought, 'I know that brotha.' Yeah. So how you been? You lookin' good. Sweet ride and all. Family doin' okay?"

"Oh yeah. Yeah. Thanks for asking. Yours?"

"Everybody's gettin' along. No complaints. My moms, she doin' alright. Things are tough sometimes, but we surviving. You know?"

"Right."

"Yeah, man, I just had a little boy not too long ago. I just left him at his mama's house. Yeah, they say dude look just like me." He beamed. "I got a little girl too. Just beautiful, man. I'm blessed."

Bradley nodded.

"You got any kids?"

"Nah. Not yet."

"Eh, man, they a blessin'. Let me tell ya. I'm feelin' blessed. Straight up, dog. You know, I went through some things there for a while. You know? Yeah, got caught up a lil' bit. But I'm gettin' it back together," he said, with a slow, steady nod. "Slowly but surely."

"Right."

"Well, look here, bruh. My ride is here. Gotta jet. You take care, though. Alright? Peace out."

"Yeah, Marcus, you too. Good seeing you, man."

He trotted to where a city bus was rolling to a stop alongside the curb. The doors opened, allowing him and another passenger to step aboard. The doors closed and it looked as though the man and woman had been gobbled up, like a fish devouring plankton, before the lumbering vehicle pulled away from the curb and swam back into the stream of traffic.

Bradley slipped into his car and headed out.

22

Flight 1310 had finally docked and Abby stood patiently waiting for the aisle to empty so she, too, could deplane. The landing had been smooth, not unlike the entire trip home. With the flight over, she was grateful to be back on the ground again. She'd made it.

As she approached the front of the airplane, Abby saw a smiling flight attendant and pilot posted at the exit like a couple of local dignitaries standing on the stage during a high school commencement.

"Thank you." "Thank you," one said after the other like a couple of androids.

Abby was tickled by the image and instantly thought of Bradley. She gave the cheerful crew a quick smile before ducking out the door.

Moments later she emerged from the passenger tunnel expecting to see Bradley standing amid the other people gathered in the waiting area to greet their loved ones. A mild sense of disappointment swept over her, feeling her long-awaited hopes had been deferred.

She hovered momentarily while the crowd thinned. Any moment she expected he would come trotting through the terminal the way it happens in the movies. When after several minutes the narrative still hadn't played out, she proceeded to the baggage claim area. As she walked—in the familiar and far less congested surroundings of the small terminal—she was completely at ease. She knew in fact where she was headed and wasn't worried a bit about being led astray or confused by an unfamiliar tongue.

Abby sat alone in an empty corner of the airport in front of a large window near the terminal's entrance. The wonder she'd experienced briefly while noticing how freshly fallen snow can alter an area's emotional landscape had all but melted away. Her dose of cozy exhilaration the first snowfall brings was slowly wearing off.

How long had she been seated there in the front window? Fifteen, maybe twenty minutes? She looked out the window once more and saw pretty much same scene as before—light traffic and a few people milling about as activity at the airport slowed to a crawl until the next plane arrival or departure.

She pondered about her fiancé's whereabouts and cracked a wry smile. C.P. time? She chuckled softly.

She resumed scanning a lifestyle magazine while the sound of some easy-listening tune oozed from a ceiling speaker. The smooth jazz ceased momentarily as a woman's voice paged the name of an unknown passenger. The mushy soprano saxophone riff promptly resumed, like a musical adaptation of an EKG display barely maintaining a pitch.

The voice-music combination reminded her of a Richard Pryor skit Bradley often imitated. After being hospitalized for a heart attack, Pryor told an audience how he awoke to the sound of soft music in a hospital room full of whites. Upon opening his eyes, his first thought was, Oh shit. I done died and been sent to the wrong Heaven. Now I got to sit and listen to Lawrence Welk for the rest of my days.

She recalled how Bradley loved that line. She also remembered being somewhat annoyed by the umpteenth time he recited it. Not long before, Abby had discovered her codename—Sweet Polly Purebred—shared among the brothers. Why are white people always characterized as so square or unhip? she had asked, dryly. Bradley replied that she couldn't be serious, as his laughter silenced and became a chicken grin.

Bradley had become such an integral part of her life. But unlike five days ago when she longed for his physical security after her arrival in exotic Miami, she now wanted his warmth, his humor, and his beauty. Thinking about what he meant to her invited thoughts of what she'd ever do without him.

As she glanced again out the window before looking at her watch once more, she realized it was a question she hadn't yet fully acknowledged. With all the talk about their future together, she never really had time to consider the possibilities if all of that talk failed to materialize. Or what if—after marriage—he died, leaving her a young widow? She wouldn't know the first thing about making funeral arrangements. Where would he be laid to rest? If he were to be deposited in the earth in this town, would she forever be tied to this place?

One evening, while she and Bradley were driving on the outskirts of town, they passed a cemetery tucked away behind a tree line and hills.

"My mom's buried over there," Bradley said, matter-of-factly.

"Oh" was all she managed to say. Some things he could be just so matter-of-fact about. Abby would later accompany him to the gravesite on Mother's Day to watch him place flowers and touch the ground where his mother lay, in a cemetery that was essentially a segregated burial ground. There was nothing about the gesture that struck her as being anything less than genuine. And because of it, her heart nearly split in two the first time she saw Bradley do it.

As she stared into the future, imagining all sorts of things, like final resting-places, she decided right then that she would never allow any husband of hers to be buried in a segregated cemetery. After all, this wasn't 1950.

"Bradley?" she whispered. "Where are you?"

Outside, the snow continued to fall.

23

Bradley had another stop to make before home.

With the gas needle pressed to E, he was running on fumes as some would say. There was at least a gallon or two left in the tank; more than enough to complete his run of errands.

Still, he could already hear Abby's subtle objection: *Why do you drive around on E so much?*

So he pulled into the station just up the road a ways from his subdivision in Grand Heights, parked at a pump island near the road, and got out.

Snow fell heavily and he squinted amid the swirl of large flakes. A trail of footprints in the fresh layer of snow followed him across the pavement as he strode toward the building.

Bradley saw a young man scurry from mini-mart to the maroon Toyota Supra with darkened windows and thought little of it. Truth be told, Bradley might have thought twice if he had come upon a black guy behaving in a like manner—hustling out of a store a bit suspiciously to a waiting automobile. His step might have hesitated and his body tensed up, if only for a blink, as he made a hyper-quick calculation on the odds of that young man being a straight-up gangsta instead of someone in a hurry who just happened to be black. But because he was white, Bradley unwittingly gave him a pass. Likely just another white suburban, make-believe hip-hopster, trying to front like a young brotha he'd met only through MTV. His so-called urban-street attire made him doubly safe; that is, clear of the racial hang-ups of his forbearers. No doubt, though, he'd be back in the mainstream fold soon enough.

So there was no dithering on Bradley's part. He walked

fearlessly into a situation that wasn't his making. It was the second man out the door of the mini-mart that froze Bradley in his tracks. This time, he knew for sure.

To the *Daily News*, a witness described it this way:

> *A girl said she saw a man come running out of the store and jump into a burgundy car. A second man then ran out of the store and fired a gun once at another man who had just driven up and was now walking toward the building.*
> *The man was felled by a blast of gunfire. The shooter then got into the burgundy car and it sped away.*

A single shot. Sometimes it only takes one.

Bradley lay on his back, breathless in the fresh snow, his head ringing from a spinning sensation. The sound around him then went dead and his vision faded. Bradley felt himself tiring very quickly.

All he wanted to do was sleep. He closed his eyes.

Bradley squirmed and grunted, like a child roused from a deep sleep by his mother—h*er smile beatific as she spoke softly: "Time to do some living."*

"Okay," he mumbled. "Okay."

He stood up, squeezing a handful of his own flesh and staggered into the mini-mart, leaving behind the faint imprint of a bloodied snow angel.

"Is everyone all right?" he cried out, through a grimaced expression. "Hey? I-I need some help."

There was no response.

Alone, Bradley stumbled out of the building and back outside where he collapsed onto the snow-covered pavement.

Abby rose quickly when she heard her name called. It was about a half-hour later than she expected.

A lone man charged forward and stopped at a distance. He only saw Abby, standing there all alone with her bags.

"I…I'm sorry that I'm late," he pushed out.

Abby looked at him, her head slightly askew. Her mouth strained to form a smile but her eyes weren't buying it.

"What?" she asked. "James? What are you doing here? Where's Brad?"

They each stepped forward, closing the distance. Words had been placed on hold as her quizzical smile was replaced with burgeoning unease.

James focused on a spot just below Abby's right ear as he moved in to embrace her. His eyes began to leak. They embraced each other.

"James? What's wrong? Where's Bradley?"

He sucked in a few heavy breaths and exhaled with great effort each time. Finally, he said: "We've got to go."

"What? Go where? Where are we going?"

"To the hospital. We need to get the hospital."

24

J ames sighed impatiently as his eyes shifted elsewhere—to a place beyond the room. He pondered that troubling question.

He recalled the day his father told them their mother went away and wouldn't be coming home ever again. The way his father withheld his personal grief in order to comfort two sobbing little boys as the coffin's lid was lowered that final time was really something, he said. Closed. The end. Never to be seen again in this life.

He explained how they hadn't always gotten along, he and his father. For a long time, he thought the old man preferred Bradley. Obedient, easier to control, Bradley the ever-reliable son who did as he was told.

"Or at least he tried to do what was asked of him," James allowed. "It amazes me sometimes how he does it."

James paused momentarily. He continued.

"Me? I was stubborn. Still am. I take things more personal. It especially upsets me when people try to insult my intelligence."

The woman said nothing.

"I guess I picked up that part of our father's personality," James said.

"How so? What do you mean?"

"I got the side of him that doesn't take any stuff. You know my father once threatened a school official—this white dude. Well, he didn't threaten him directly."

"Tell me about that," said the therapist, an older woman who struck him as kind of cute. "What happened exactly?"

"Well, we had been bused over to a different junior high school in a lily-white part of town. You know, for integration. And I did not feel welcomed. Nope, I just did not feel welcomed. I did not want to be there. Me and my boys did not want to be there. Not that things were happening on a daily basis. I mean, there were some fights early on and a lot of talk and that sort of thing. Mostly, a lot of talk. You know, occasionally you'd see stuff like, 'I hate niggers' or 'go back to Africa' scribbled in the bathroom stalls. But we'd laugh about it, especially when saw the word 'nigger' misspelled. Every now and then, you'd see the word 'niger' written somewhere—you know, spelled with only one 'g'—and I'd think, *these idiots can't even spell.*"

He chuckled; she cracked a dim smile.

"Mostly, though," he said, becoming serious again, "it was just an atmosphere where you felt like everything related to you was an afterthought or forced. It didn't feel right or natural. I felt like some kind of guinea pig."

"Mm."

"You had teachers who found it very easy to ignore you or were amazed if you could add straight. The stuff we did that was out of line was treated differently if white boys did the same kind of thing. The hall guards could be a trip. They were more familiar with the white students because they lived in the same neighbourhoods and what not. You know, I didn't like their music. You see, we had come from an all-black elementary school where you felt like the teachers really cared if you messed up. I can appreciate that now—where they were coming from. Maybe not so much then. But now I can."

"You mean the black teachers at your elementary school?"

"Right. We had some white teachers, too," he added quickly, as if to say he wasn't marooned in Bronzeville without any connection whatsoever outside of it. "The funny thing is, though, I, we, didn't necessarily see those teachers as white. They were part of the community. You know?"

James paused as though he had just stumbled upon something unexpectedly. He scanned the volumes of books on her shelves. His mind drifted back to his grandparents' house as he recalled how his grandmother would store mementos—a dried, flattened carnation; an old photograph; a small 'thank you' card or some other heartfelt note; a slip of paper with no clear value—in the pages of different books. It could be like finding buried treasure. *Maybe they were just makeshift bookmarks stuck in stories to be continued*, he later thought.

The therapist was silent.

"We used to have assemblies for Black History Month and everything. But they did jive shit like Fifties' Day where you were supposed to dress up like Richie, Joanie or Potsy. Me and my boys were like later for that BS."

"Why?"

"You know what the Fifties were like for black people in this country?"

She stared.

"It sure as hell wasn't *Happy Days*. I mean, what we were supposed to do? Move to the back of the bus? Hold a civil rights demonstration? Shoot, for all I know, they may have started talking about lynching somebody. Maybe I should have gone as Emmett Till. Now wouldn't that have been a trip?"

The woman blinked into a tight smile.

"I just didn't like the environment. We were always outnumbered. Always. You know, we had this intramural hoop team in the seventh grade. It was made up of some fellas from the 'hood."

"Was your brother on the team?"

"No. He didn't play sports. He was in band. Anyway, we were all seventh graders. It was a seventh-grade division. Anyway, we waxed every other seventh-grade team at the school—waxed 'em—and even beat a couple of eighth-grade teams. We were undefeated. Yeah, we made it all the way to the city finals in our division. But, you know, we didn't get any support from the school. No pats on the back. Nothing in the school paper. No P.A. announcement. Nothing. Nada. And here we were representing our school, which had never had any good sports teams before we arrived, except maybe in baseball. That didn't count in our world."

"Did your father come see you play?"

"No. No, he had to work." He looked away briefly.

"Mm-hmm...So did you guys win the city championship?"

"Naw. We got blew out by some brothas from a school on the northside," he chuckled, lost in reminiscence. "Yeah, we got shook by something like thirty points. One of the dudes we played against is in the NBA now."

"So you were up against a pretty talented group of guys?"

"Uh, yeah," he chuckled. "But they had a coach too. We were just run-'n-gun, out there having fun."

James could tell she didn't quite understand what he meant by "run-'n-gun" but felt no obligation to explain himself.

"Mm-hmm. So, what about the incident involving your father and the school official. Tell me about that."

"Right. Me and some partners were messing around in a bathroom one day, you know, talking and stuff. So one of my friends started bouncing a basketball off the mirror. I know, I know. It was stupid," he said, as if reliving the lesson drilled into him from days long past. "But, if you did it fast enough, it created this weird illusion of playing catch with yourself, like you were throwing the ball and catching it at the same time. So we all took turns tripping over this illusion. The faster you went, the quicker you had to be. You ever see one of those cartoons where the quarterback throws a pass and then runs down field and catches it himself?"

"Mm. Like you were faster than a speeding bullet, huh?"

James' eyes were flinty in the moment of silence that followed; never once removing his gaze from her. He felt his right eye twitch slightly.

"Yeah," he said, finally, "just like Superman…Then all of a sudden, the mirror broke. But it didn't just crack. It shattered to the floor. Crash! And it was loud as hell. You know, with all that tile and porcelain and metal, I didn't think that sound would ever stop echoing in my ears. Before we could scat, a hall guard was on the scene with the quickness."

"What happened then?"

"He. Was. Pissed. He wanted to know what was going on. We told him it was an accident. Then he said, 'Trying to make this place feel like home? Well, maybe you boys can do that over in your neighbourhood, but not over here. We take care of our things in this neighbourhood.' We were like: *What? This old ass school?*"

"He said that?"

"Yup, like we were a bunch of uncivilized little niggas who had come over to tear-up their fucking school in Honkyville. 'Scuse my language. Then they wanted to kick us out of school for vandalism and what not," his voice becoming singsong. "My father went to the school to keep me from getting kicked out."

"Had you told him what the hall monitor said?"

"Yes I did. I told him. And he told the principal that he didn't appreciate his son and his friends being talked to in that way. That he works hard every day, every single day, like his father and mother had before him. And that his son and his friends were good boys who knew right from wrong. He demanded an apology and warned that the hall guard would have to deal with him directly the next time he said something like that to me. Basically, Pops' attitude was, 'Let him say that shit to my face.' Pardon my French. Anyway, I thought that was cool. Yeah."

"So you were present when your father spoke to the principal?"

"Yes, ma'am."

She stared at James momentarily before speaking. "Did he, or you, get an apology?"

"The principal apologized and said he would look into the comments that were made."

"You think the principal did what he said he would do?"

"I dunno and didn't care, really. Besides, I still got put on punishment for being in the bathroom that day messin' around. So. There you go."

Despite all that, James had still harbored some bitterness toward the man because he hadn't been around more often. When they were together, he wasn't always the same easy-going barber customers chatted with at the shop. There were two sides to Ellis Cunningham, and James didn't know which one was for real. The youngest son pledged privately he was gone for good after he shipped out with the Marines.

Bradley was his bridge back to that place in which he'd grown up, the one he'd struggled to make sense of and figure out where he belonged. Not just brothers from afar during those intervening years, they were pen pals. Bradley's early letters was a recurring voice from the other side; the one heard from atop the army climbing wall—*You can do this, Jay. You got this. Dad really misses you (me, too)*—that urged him on.

Gradually, the exchanges became part of a long-running chess match of sorts, as one pondered his opponent's move and plotted his own. The handwritten correspondences were life sustaining and far better than the occasional transoceanic phone calls because they allowed for greater absorption of the content. Words and meanings were conveyed that were rarely spoken, if ever, and they always seemed to arrive at the right time.

James was glad to be back at home, though he didn't stay under Ellis' roof for long after his discharge from the service.

Bradley was already gone, he said. He, too, had become his own man.

"You know, back when this all started…"

He stopped talking and looked down at his clasped hands resting in his lap. After an extended pause, James drew in a deep breath and changed course.

"I've always looked up to my brother. I don't think that I've ever told anyone that before," he said. "B had always been there for me, to help pull me through. *Always.* In some ways, I feel like I was able to figure some things out just by watching him—how he managed things and was able to channel his energy elsewhere. I feel like there's so much more that I don't know and that I need to know."

James stopped talking and looked the woman squarely in the face.

"After he was, um, shot, and we were gathered at the hospital, I remembered: *Oh, shit! Abby!* Bradley was supposed to pick up Abby from the airport that day. So I left to go get her and brought her back to be with the family."

"That must've been incredibly difficult for you; for you both, actually."

"Yeah, it was…It was." James chuckled. "You know, I used to call her Polly."

"Polly?"

"Yeah. She hated it; said it was disrespectful, and I have much respect for Abby. Believe that; much respect for her," he said, accented with a slow, affirmative nod. "Abby never said anything to me about it, though. After a while I think she realized that I really didn't mean anything by it. It was a way to poke at my brother a little bit, I guess."

"Mm. So why did you call her Polly?"

He chuckled, sheepishly. "Well, it's kind of a long story."

That story would have to wait, as the woman, without ever

glancing at her watch, announced that their time was just about up.

"Before I let you go: How is Bradley?"

"Better. Much better. He's getting better every day." James paused as he looked out the window. "You know, growing up, people, some friends of mine used to think that Bradley didn't know what time it is…um, I mean like he wasn't cool; like he didn't know what's going on. Humph. He's a tough guy. Yeah. We're blessed…Anyway, he and Abby, they're finally tying the knot this fall. I'm the best man."

She smiled as they sat there in silence. "Okay, then. So would you like to set another appointment to continue with our discussions, or what?"

After a moment of hesitation, James replied, "Yes, I'd like that."

"Okay. Just one moment. Let me grab my appointment book," she said. "How does two weeks from today sound? That would be the twenty-second."

"Yeah," he said. "That'll work."

"That's good?"

"Yup."

"Okay. See you then." She smiled.

James sat motionless, though his eyes wandered about.

Outside, billowy white clouds crowded the midday sky. The bundles of tiny water droplets and ice crystals moved briskly as though they were chariots racing across the heavens.

Inside, James once again trained his eyes on her.

"All right," he said, "until next time."

James smiled softly and rose from the worn, cloth sofa, and left the office after a quick good-bye. As he strode across the parking lot to his car. He didn't cower against the cold wind grating his face. He resisted the urge to hunch over because he could get through it faster simply by walking straight.

Once inside the car, he let it warm up a bit before dropping in a cassette tape—one that Bradley had given him some time ago. He then pulled out the ashtray and retrieved a half-smoked joint before pressing in the car's lighter. Once the heater lighter popped out, James lit the joint and took a few hits as he sat in the idling car.

Plastic people with plastic minds are on their way to plastic homes

No beginning there ain't no ending just on and on and on and on
and on, it'sAll because they're so afraid to say that they're alone
Until our hero rides in, rides in on his saxophone.
Could you call on Lady Day,
Could you call on John Coltrane
Now 'cause they'll,
They'll wash your troubles,
Your troubles, your troubles
Your troubles away!

He took another hit before flicking the smoldering roach out the car's lowered window. He revved the car's engine and shifted into gear.

James pulled out of the parking lot and made a left turn into traffic. He headed back into town to go home.

Acknowledgments

This book is the product of many long nights, frustrating days, and bouts with self-doubt. The long-term love affair also delivered the highest of highs throughout, none more so than the email received early one November morning from Urban Farmhouse Press, stating that Motown Man had been accepted for publication. So, I am extremely grateful to publisher Daniel Lockhart for his belief in the story. I also must thank fiction editor Maeve Keating for her careful editing of the manuscript, along with Daniel's.

My drive toward publication was aided by friends, fellow writers and editors, and family, whom I wish to thank. I want to thank beta reader and editor Sharon Umbaugh for helping to shape my manuscript without silencing my voice. A big thanks to Scott Atkinson, too, for selecting my essay for Happy Anyway: A Flint Anthology, which he edited. The publication re-lit my pilot light for creative writing. Editors/writers John Haggerty, Christine Maul Rice, Anna Clark, Anne Trubek, Martha Bayne, Ryan Schnurr and Jordan Heller have been tremendously helpful along the way, keeping the fire burning.

I want to thank the individual members of Flint Festival of Writers committee – Connor Coyne, Jan Worth Nelson, Sarah Carson, Katie Curnow and James Schirmer – for their dedication to the literary craft and support in the run-up to publication.

Special thanks to my two English teachers at Flint Southwestern High School: Mrs. Foster (who once wrote in the margins of a research paper I'd written, "You write quite well.") and Mrs. Abrams, who stirred my interest in great literature.

My siblings Gail, Clarence Jr., Madeline (deceased), Carole and

Cheryl, and niece/'sister' Dionne have all been instrumental in my development as a writer, storyteller and person. Thank you for your love and support. It means more to me than I have ever said aloud. To long-time, dear friends Elton Walker and Myron Tucker: Man, y'all are like brothers to me.

Thank you to my wife, Wanda, for your love, patience, believing in my dreams and challenging me to remember the reader; and my son, Jonathan whose calm resolve and confidence moves me to no end.

And to my parents, the late Clarence and Rose Campbell, whose work ethic, aspirations, humor and love of the open road continue to stir my imagination, I say, "Thank you for everything. I really wish you were here to be able to place a copy on the bookshelf and then to see your smiles."

Bob

About the Author

Bob Campbell is a writer based in Flint, Michigan. He worked as an electrician at AC Spark Plug and later a staff writer for the *Flint Journal*, the *Lexington Herald-Leader*, and the *Detroit Free Press*. He grew up in the Elm Park neighborhood on the south side of Flint.